The Defender

·THE·NEWBERY·HONOR·ROLL·

The Defender

Nicholas Kalashnikoff

Illustrations by
Claire Louden and George Louden, Jr.

Troll Associates

TO
MY DAUGHTER

This edition published in the United States of America in 1993 by Walker Publishing Company, Inc.

Published simultaneously in Canada by Thomas Allen & Son Canada, Limited, Markham, Ontario

Library of Congress Cataloging-in-Publication Data
Kalashnikoff, Nicholas.
The defender / Nicholas Kalashnikoff: illustrations by Claire Louden and George Louden, Jr.
p. cm. —(The Newbery honor roll)
Summary: Turgen, a shepherd in northeastern Siberia, defends the wild mountain rams and befriends a widow and her children.
ISBN 0-8027-7397-4
[1. Siberia (Russia)—Fiction. 2. Rams—Fiction.] I. Louden, Claire, ill. II. Louden, George, ill. III. Title. IV. Series.
PZ7.K12348De 1993
[Fic]—dc20 92-33560
CIP
AC

Printed in the United States of America
2 3 4 5 6 7 8 9 10

PREFACE

"Everywhere there is life, and everywhere there are warm human hearts." These words, spoken by a schoolteacher, I remember from many years ago when I was a boy in Siberia. The teacher, Ivan Pavin, was a man who took joy in his work and passed joy on to his pupils. The world was a more wonderful place for discovering it with him. Best of all, he delighted to tell us about people—all kinds of people—but especially those of northern Siberia who lived in never-ending conflict with a harsh land.

When I grew up and left the village, I spent several years in the Far North, where I had many occasions to test the truth of this saying. Yes—I found warm hearts in plenty, but none warmer than that of Tim, who was of the Yakut tribe. Tim's full name was Timofey. He was greatly respected by people among whom he lived, not only because he was honest and brave but because he had powerful fists to match his courage. When words *failed to convince, his fists often could. One thing about him interested me in particular. He was a self-appointed champion of the* chubuku, *or wild mountain rams, and took every opportunity to plead with hunters to spare these rare animals who were fast disappearing from the region.*

"Why?" I asked him one day, upon hearing him threaten to punish a hunter who dared kill a ram in that neighborhood. "Why do you put yourself out to befriend these creatures? Are they so precious to you?"

"Why?" he repeated my question. "That is simple. My step-father, Turgen, who was a Lamut, loved the mountain rams, and I made him a promise to protect them after he was gone. He is dead now—a fine man, as anyone will tell you. Perhaps you would like to hear about him."

I assured him that I would. . . .

CHAPTER 1

THIS IS THE STORY OF THE LAMUT, TURGEN, who lived alone high in the hills of northeastern Siberia and had for friends a herd of mountain rams.

Turgen, whose name means "fleet-of-foot" in the Lamut tongue, was a lonely man. It had not always been so. When he was younger he had had a wife and a son whom he loved. But both had died of an illness that burned like fire, and rested now in a single grave under the larch tree outside his door. He had also had the liking and trust of the Yakuts who were his neighbors in the valley below. Among them he was famed for his knowledge of medicine. Knowing him for a kindly, generous man, they came to him for healing grasses, and were never refused. He, in turn, visited them and sat by their *komeleks*, or fire-places, to exchange the latest news.

All this was in the past. Turgen no longer received callers

or went into the valley, except to take fish to the widow Marfa and receive milk for his own use. Marfa and her two children, a son Tim and a daughter Aksa, were Turgen's only friends. For the most part he stayed close to his *yurta,* a simple hut perched between two cliffs above a mountain stream. On sunny days, when he was not hunting or fishing, he loved to sit on a rough bench under a great larch tree and smoke his pipe while watching the activity in the valley below. The mountains were full of mystery and peace. Because of them he could think of the past without regret.

You wonder why the people of the valley shunned Turgen. The reason, you will say, was no reason at all. Word had spread among them that he was friendly with the wild rams who lived in the mountains. "Who ever heard of friendship between a man and mountain rams?" the Yakuts asked. It was impossible. And if it was impossible, then Turgen was a sorcerer—a partner of the devil.

CHAPTER 2

G OSSIP, STARTING LIKE A SMALL FIRE, GOT
bigger and bigger. One occasion especially
helped this evil rumor. On a holiday, years
before, the people of the valley had gathered to eat and
drink and dance. As always, the shamanist was present—a
man believed to have power to communicate with the
good and evil spirits who were part of an ancient faith.
And as always he ate and drank with the gayest of the
company.

The shamanist had long been jealous of Turgen because
of his influence over the Yakuts. For one thing, Turgen was
a sober man and kept his wits at all times, which the
shamanist did not do. As the shamanist was dependent
upon voluntary contributions for his living, he could not
tolerate the thought of yielding any authority to another.

On this day the party went on hour after hour, until the
shamanist from an excess of food, drink, and excitement

fell down unconscious. To the superstitious Yakuts, who revered him greatly, he was in a trance and they waited eagerly to hear what he would report about his conversation with the spirits when he awoke.

A woman named Stepa went to him and wailed:

"Arise, O Shamanist, and open our eyes, ignorant people that we are. Tell us our future and what we have to fear."

In a short while the shamanist rose, looked about him with wild eyes, seized his tambourine and struck it several times.

"I saw," he muttered, "I saw a dark cloud swim across the sky to Turgen's yurta. I looked. I looked, and in it was the figure of a devil. A real devil, with horns and a tail like a cow's. I spoke, putting a spell upon him, and he changed into a wild ram. I made the spell stronger, and he vanished in the exact spot where Turgen lives. O my friends! Beware of the devil in the ram's hide!"

With that, the shamanist fell to the ground again exhausted.

Amazed, the Yakuts said to one another, "He has seen the devil! Let us be thankful that the devil passed us by and went instead after the soul of Turgen."

But here the woman Stepa, who wanted to be in the shamanist's good graces, interrupted. "Beware the devil!"

she screamed. "He can come to you too. You say that Turgen is a Christian—but has anyone seen him pray when the priest visited us? No. Believe me, the devil is looking to have such people for a friend. Beware of Turgen! Avoid him!"

The Yakuts were more impressed by the shamanist's vision than by Stepa's words. Still they listened and remembered. When, not long afterwards, the shamanist had another vision in which Turgen was associating with the devil, the simple started to believe. They did not condemn Turgen, nor would they harm him. "If he has bound himself to the devil," they said, "that is his affair. We'll just stay away from him."

They did so, and time passed. People might even have forgotten the story of Turgen's sorcery had not a simple, foolish man named Nikita come running to the village one day to report in great excitement that he had seen Turgen sitting on the bench beneath his larch tree while a mountain ram strolled nearby.

"With my own eyes I saw it," he declared. "A wild ram in company with a man."

Everyone knew Nikita for a careless talker who embroidered truth with a lively imagination, but the Yakuts were a superstitious people and like many others were easily convinced by loud shouting. "Think of it," they said, shaking their heads dolefully, "a wild ram has become tame. Such a thing has never been heard of before. This really smells of the devil's work."

For these men had hunted the mountain rams all their lives and they knew no wild creature in the world was so fearful of human beings. Hunting them was hazardous sport because the rams lived in the most remote crags. Many a hunter had fallen and been crippled for life trying to search them out. There was a saying that anyone who killed a ram was certain to meet misfortune, but this was one of those popular beliefs not to be examined too carefully for truth.

Of course, the Yakuts might have gone to Turgen and questioned him, but they didn't. "Is it reasonable to ask a sorcerer why he takes the devil for friend?" they asked. "Better stay out of harm's way lest the evil spirits reach out and take the inquisitive ones also into their net."

So it was that the people of the valley no longer visited Turgen, or he them.

CHAPTER 3

"WORDS THAT SPEAK EVIL, THOUGH they have no teeth, can tear the heart," was an old proverb. It hurt Turgen that the Yakuts turned from him, avoided his questions and all contact with him. It was as if a dead wall of ill-will had suddenly risen between him and the people of the valley. Because he was ignorant of any wrong on his part, he tried not to think too much and went about his own affairs. But solitude is not easy to endure, for the reason that thoughts cannot be trapped. They keep buzzing round and round in the head, like angry autumn flies, giving one no rest.

Turgen thought of himself as independent, healthy and strong and in need of no one's assistance. Still it was difficult to be deprived of human talk and human association.

Fortunately for him, there lived in the valley a widow named Marfa with her two children—a boy Tim and a girl

Aksa—at whose komelek he was welcome to sit whenever it pleased him. There he would smoke his pipe and entertain the children with some story, and on leaving hear the warm and comforting words: "Come again Turgen, and soon."

Marfa owned a good cow which furnished milk sufficient for her own needs and for her friend. Turgen loved hot tea with milk, to him a real treat.

Marfa's yurta stood near a lake which was surrounded by a forest, far from other dwellings. The Yakuts seldom visited her. Knowing that she was poor, they feared she might ask something of them, and because of the children they might be moved to rash promises. Conscience has a way of making itself felt, like a thorn in the body, so they reasoned that it would be safer to stay away and avoid temptation.

Marfa would have considered herself poor indeed had she not had a solid yurta and her fine cow. But one cannot live on milk alone. Necessity forced her to leave the children by day and work for some wealthy Yakuts. Her heart was never at ease with the children alone at home, but she had no choice.

Hers was not an easy life. In the summer she caught fish by nets from the lake, mowed the field grass to feed the cow in winter, made clothes for the children, and saw to it that there was firewood stored away for the cold weather. Trees were abundant, but it was beyond her strength to chop them down, and she had no horse with which to drag the logs out of the woods. So, in return for housework, her Yakut employer chopped and delivered wood for her. In spite of work and worry, she did not complain. She asked nothing of God, except good health for herself, her children, and her cow. God must have seen and been pleased, for all of them were blessed with the best of health.

The cow lived in a warm shed separated from the yurta by a thin partition which in summer opened like a window to admit her head. There she would stand chewing her cud and regarding everybody with her kind eyes. No wonder that she was considered a welcome member of the family. The children carried on long conversations with her, not in the least frightened by her great size and magnificent horns. They knew her to be good-natured and fully believed that she understood everything they said. Maybe she did. It is certain that she knew her name, Whitey, for she answered to it promptly when called. In the grazing season the children were charged to look after her lest she stray too far, but Marfa sometimes wondered whether it was not Whitey who guarded the children. In many ways her cow sense prompted her that her help was necessary if Tim and Aksa were to grow up well and strong, and she gave it gladly.

These were Turgen's friends in the valley, a kindly family but poor.

CHAPTER 4

A PERSON WHO IS ALONE SPENDS A GREAT deal of time in thought. It was so with Turgen. And though his thoughts repeated themselves day after day, still he found pleasure in them. True, they got mixed up at times, so that he found it difficult to separate present from past: all appeared part of one precious experience, without beginning or end. But whichever way his thoughts turned—there were Marfa and the children.

They had become his friends shortly after the death of Marfa's husband. Turgen had known the couple for years, but acquaintance is not the same as friendship.

He remembered Marfa when she was a frightened girl working in the homes of wealthy Yakuts. At that time he had no occasion to speak to her, and besides she was very shy. Then when she was past her first youth she married a Yakut in the neighborhood who needed a good worker to look after his three cows. Marfa's life was changed by marriage but it was not improved. Her husband was a sickly man unable to do a full day's work, and when the children came her cares increased. The death of the husband soon after the birth of their second child left Marfa with the burden of the household upon her. Of the three cows, two had to be sold. Hardships and the years put wrinkles in her face and she grew old before her time. However, her body was fortunately still strong and she accepted what God sent.

This part of her life Turgen knew only from hearsay. It was later that he met her as a friend, and he loved to recall the incident.

One winter, returning from a hunt on skis, he was passing her yurta when he noticed that neither sparks nor smoke came from the chimney. He stopped at once, thinking in fright, "A dead chimney. What has happened? I must investigate."

To people of the North a chimney without life in the cold of winter is a sign of disaster.

Turgen ran towards the yurta. While still some distance away he could hear the anxious mooing of the cow and a child weeping. He opened the door cautiously. The yurta was dark and cold.

"Who is it? Come in and help me light a fire," a childish voice called. Turgen struck a match and saw a small boy, his face and hands black with soot, rocking a cradle in which a baby sat crying as if the world were lost. With his free hand he tried to stir the fire in the komelek into life while he blew on its dead embers.

"Let me," Turgen said, and added, "Don't be afraid of me. But I can see that you are a big boy and not easily frightened."

"Yes," the boy answered soberly. "Mama says that I am already five and Aksa is two winters old. She is little and an awful cry-baby. My name is Tim. What is yours?"

"My name is Turgen. I like you, Tim."

"I like you, too."

Then, examining Turgen by the light of the new dancing fire, he said, "Why should I be afraid of you? You built the fire, so you must be kind."

"Where is your mother?" Turgen asked.

"She went to work and I was to keep up the fire. But I slept and the fire died," the boy admitted guiltily.

The yurta was now warm and cheerful. Both the cow and the baby had stopped their crying. The little girl could not take her bright, inquisitive eyes away from the strange man.

While taking off his kuklianka Turgen questioned the boy. "Is the cow hungry that she was calling so? And what about your sister?"

Tim shrugged his shoulders. "Our cow always moos like that when there is no fire in the komelek. She is afraid for us. And Aksa must be hungry. Mama told me to give her milk with hot water to drink, but how could I heat the water when there was no fire?"

"Of course," Turgen agreed. "That wasn't your fault. I'll do it right away."

Having had her warm milk, Aksa was soon sitting on Turgen's knees looking with drowsy and contented eyes into the leaping fire. The visitor pleased her as well as Tim.

Happy to have their trust, Turgen considered what other help he could give them. "Have you any flour, meat and fish?" he asked the boy.

Tim shook his head. "Mama said that there is a little barley meal, but no meat or fish. She will ask the neighbors for some. Perhaps you are hungry. I will give you half of my mill-cake. Do you want it?"

"No, thank you, Tim. I am not hungry. Besides, there is smoked uikola in my bag. Do you like it?"

"Very much. It is fat. Aksa also loves it, and Mama too. Give some to them."

"I shall give you all that I have and later I'll bring you more."

Turgen was enjoying his conversation with the bright little boy. "Tell me, who taught you how to keep the fire going in the komelek?"

"Mama," said Tim promptly. "She says that if you blow on the hot coals they will flare up. But no matter how hard I blew, nothing happened. We have matches but Mama hides them from me. She is afraid I might set the yurta on fire."

Aksa was ready to sleep now, so Turgen wrapped a blanket around her and put her in the basket, which served as a crib. Then he examined the yurta.

Poverty stared at him from every corner. Nowhere could he see a sign of food. "I will come tomorrow and bring more fish," he promised himself, "for I have plenty of everything."

"When do you expect your mother?" he asked Tim.

"Soon. She never lets us stay alone in the dark, and it is almost evening. Maybe she got a lot of fish and it is heavy for her to carry," he suggested.

"Perhaps. But sit up until she comes, and keep the fire going. In weather like this it is easy to freeze without a fire." He picked up his kuklianka. "Now I must be going.

Tell your mother that the Lamut Turgen was here. She knows me."

The boy looked at Turgen with eyes which begged him to stay. "I like to watch the fire . . . when I am not alone. You know how to do everything, don't you? When I grow up I will know everything too, just like you. Please don't go for a while."

"I must," Turgen told him. "I live in the mountains and want to be home before it gets too dark. It is good that you are not the cowardly sort."

"Why must you get home before dark?" Tim wanted to know. "Are you afraid of wolves? I hear they attack people in winter. But you have a gun. What kind is it? A good one?"

Turgen threw back his head and laughed. "Oh, what a talker! You know about wolves and even guns. Someday you'll surely be a hunter. And now, good-by. Mind you don't fall asleep. I'll be back soon."

CHAPTER 5

NIGHT COMES QUICKLY IN THE NORTH, SO Turgen walked briskly. His heart was troubled as he thought of the children. Only extreme want could have forced Marfa to leave them alone. For the closest neighbor, he knew, lived not less than half a mile away.

"Poor woman! Here I have everything and she nothing. It is necessary to help her. But how?"

Arriving home, he was moved by a sudden impulse to fill a sack full of frozen fish and partridges. Then, grabbing up some salt and tea, he started back to Marfa's. So high were his spirits, he did not feel the weight of his load. As his skis carried him swiftly down hill, he could see from a distance bright sparks flying from the yurta's chimney.

"The boy is not sparing with the wood. That is good." Then it occurred to him: "But maybe Marfa is home by now." The thought abashed him, for he reasoned: "Suppose she refuses my gift and says 'I am not a pauper that I should accept charity'?" And it was possible that she shared the distrust of the valley people toward him.

At the door he stood for some time hesitating. Finally he decided: "Be what may. I will say that I have no money, but I wish to buy milk from her and will pay for it with these foodstuffs." Nevertheless, he set the sack outside the door before he knocked timidly.

Marfa's voice said, "Who's there? Come in."

As he stepped over the threshold the boy cried out in joy: "It is he, Mama. The kind man who built the fire and gave us the uikola. I told you he would return."

Marfa looked at Turgen, saw that he was embarrassed, and held out her hand in greeting. "Don't mind Tim. Take off your kuklianka and come sit by the fire. Thank you for what you did for the children. I was working and was delayed. It always worries me to leave them alone, but what can I do?"

Moving quickly, she placed a tea kettle on the fire, brought out a small table and said: "Move closer to the fire and the light. Have some hot tea with mill-cakes and the uikola you gave us. You are welcome to all there is. Tomorrow they have promised to pay me in fish. My last year's catch was very poor and I have nothing left, although it is only January."

Marfa spoke simply, but her voice was charged with anxiety.

Squatting before the fire, Turgen took out his pipe and with his bare fingers picked up a burning ember with which to light it. He inhaled deeply, then let his breath go. From behind the screen of smoke he looked at Marfa attentively.

Now it came to him for the first time that he really did not know her at all. She was a thin woman of medium height, quick and determined in her movements. Her face had the prominent cheek bones and flattened nose of the Yakut. While she was not pretty, she was pleasing to look at with her dark, thick hair and hazel eyes full of kindness. "There is beauty of soul in her eyes," thought Turgen, "but sorrow too." He imagined he could read in them the truth she tried to hide: "If tomorrow I don't get anything, I really don't know what will become of us. You can see for yourself how poorly we live."

At a loss how to console her, and embarrassed by his own distress, Turgen turned to Tim as a safe subject of conversation. "You know, you have a fine son, Marfa. He was generous enough to offer me half of his mill-cake. He should be a great help to you."

"Well," Marfa answered hesitantly, "but it will take time. However, the young do grow up fast. If only God will give me the strength to raise them and put them on their feet." Then she added more cheerfully, "Do sit down. We'll have some tea. Everything is ready."

Feeling bolder and more at ease now, Turgen said, "Thank you, I will. Only permit me to give you a present. It is right outside the door."

Without waiting for her reply, he got the sack of provisions and brought it into the yurta.

"Mama, Mama," Tim cried, "now you don't have to go to work. Look at all the food he brought us!"

Marfa leaned against the wall and her eyes filled with tears. Turgen was more embarrassed than ever. But before he could think what to say or what to do, Marfa recovered her composure and thanked him warmly. "My husband used to tell me that the Yakuts avoided you because you lived in the mountains and . . . were friendly with wild rams. He also said that you were kind and that the people stupidly spread false tales about you. Now I can see this for myself. Sit down. Do. Talk to Tim while I go to prepare a real dinner."

That was an unforgettable evening for Turgen. Though few words were exchanged, he felt that much had been communicated because the hours held so much of friendship and hospitality. Tim was long alseep by the time he was ready to leave.

It had not been difficult to persuade Marfa to supply him with milk in return for provisions. "To tell you the truth," he said, "I have so much food that it will take care of all of us. And I need your milk. I used to get milk from the valley people, but now as you know they do not approve of me. I am sorry about this, and I should be more than sorry if they caused you any trouble because of your kindness to me."

Marfa's voice was firm as she answered him: "You are my friend, Turgen. You are saving my children and me from want and perhaps starvation. Who can forbid me to choose my own friends? Do not fear. I will look out for myself. Before I was timid, but now I am a mother and in my home I am mistress."

So Turgen's friendship with Marfa and her family began. In the next four years, until Tim was nine and Aksa six, it grew and flourished. "Surely God Himself directed my footsteps to their yurta," Turgen would often think.

All would have been well, except that the evil let loose in the valley was spreading and the feeling of the people against him grew and grew.

CHAPTER 6

FROM MARFA, TURGEN LEARNED WHAT HIS neighbors thought of him and said of him. Although he cared, he was a proud man and did not think it necessary to justify his actions to anyone. Furthermore, he was discovering that solitude can be a very pleasant thing. Now that visitors no longer came with their trifling requests, he had time to enjoy his small kingdom. Here he had lived all his life and he loved it—the mountains with their strange enchantment, the brook, the lake, the forest, the simple yurta. And always there was with him the memory of the wife and son his love and knowledge had not been able to save though he tried every art at his command. The flowers he had planted on their grave bloomed each summer and beckoned him on warm days to sit there on his bench with his pipe for company.

Turgen was one of those lean, muscular men to whom the years are kind. His coppery skin, so free of hair, was finely wrinkled under the narrow, kindly eyes, deepset beneath bushy brows. His gray hair grew in untidy rows like a neglected field. But his hands kept their firmness, his eyes their sharpness, his feet the spring of youth. How old was he? Impossible to say, for he had stopped reckoning the years when he reached fifty. "Why count the winters?" he asked himself. "You live through them, and thank God. For whom is it necessary to know?"

In short, Turgen looked like what he was—a kindly man, built to endure the life of a hunter and fisherman. In both these pursuits he was very skillful. And he was not poor, though many considered him so because he owned neither horses nor cows. No one is really poor who can have food for the taking, and Turgen had besides valuable pelts which were ready exchange for cartridges, yarn for nets, barley-meal, salt, and other provisions supplied by a merchant who called once a month. Kamov was the merchant's name. His visits gave Turgen much pleasure, for he brought news of the world and was always ready for a friendly chat.

What he got from the merchant Turgen shared with Marfa and her children. It was a holiday for him just to sit in her yurta sipping tea and saying nothing. To Marfa he had little to talk about, but with the children he talked freely of many things—mostly of the life around them, and of his boyhood. When the children, full of curiosity, wanted to know more and more, and questioned him about other marvels he knew, he told them tales to make their eyes grow big—tales of the great warrior Tugan and his son Chaal, a famous athlete; stories of the animals and fish who inhabited the tundra; legends explaining the sun and moon and stars. The sun, it seemed, was servant to the Great Spirit, a powerful warrior clothed in armor of precious stones and wearing a crown of fire. The moon was his sister and one of her duties was to guard the stars, those eyes of countless angels, to make sure they did not go out and plunge the world into darkness.

Yes, Turgen knew everything.

These evenings were rare. In winter he did not call for his milk oftener than twice a month but spent the long evenings weaving his nets or smoking his pipe while he stared into the fire and reflected on the odd turns that life takes, on the joys that he knew in the peace of his mountains. Or if the solitude became a burden, he would take down from a shelf a reed he had carved long ago from a willow tree. And placing it to his lips he would bring forth a sweet, sad melody that would express thoughts impossible to put in words.

After that he would lie down to sleep like a marmot, covered snugly under two blankets made of the skins of rabbits and wolves. If he was fortunate, he would be carried off in dreams to another and happier life. What he liked best was to dream of his wife and son, to re-live the fine times they had together. But to his regret nice dreams were few, the winters long and stern.

CHAPTER 7

THE MOUNTAIN RAMS HAD BECOME A PART OF Turgen's life almost by accident. It all began so long ago that he never gave thought to it until one day Marfa out of curiosity asked him a question which brought to mind an almost forgotten incident.

"Why do they call them rams?" she wanted to know. "Are not they the same as sheep?"

"Yes and no," Turgen answered. "In the family of domestic sheep only the males have horns. But all wild rams have horns. Of course, those of the female rams are smaller."

Marfa nodded. "But is it not strange that only recently you came to love the rams? Surely you knew them before."

"Of course I knew them. When I was young I used to hunt them."

"You killed them?" Aksa asked in a shocked voice.

"I did," Turgen admitted. "It was a sin. Unfortunately,

one has to live many years to understand what is good and what evil. Living alone is a help to thinking, and often something will happen to open a man's eyes."

He paused, got up and put wood on the fire, sat down again and puffed on his pipe.

"Let me tell you what happened to me twenty or more years ago. It was winter. November. Government officials called to order me to act as guide to an important foreigner, a hunter. The man was impressive—tall and stern and clean-shaven. I couldn't understand a word he said but an interpreter explained that he had come to hunt our mountain rams. I wasn't very anxious to go with him, but what could I do? The authorities insisted.

"Well, I led them up the mountain. A hunt—pah! It was a picnic. There were about twenty people in the party, including Russian and Yakut officials. There was so much to eat and drink that soon all were acting as if they were insane—shooting at everything and anything until the hills echoed with their noise. One thing I must admit though. They had excellent guns."

Tim ventured an observation. "With such guns they undoubtedly killed many animals."

Turgen's smile was contemptuous. "No. How could they? They couldn't even aim straight. In two weeks they killed two wolves, ten rabbits, and one bear they roused out of his lair. As for rams, I confess that I was crafty and led them places where rams were usually not to be found. Yet a family of five did appear suddenly out of nowhere. O, Lord, what firing there was! They all fired at once, seized by greed. And somehow they managed to kill the largest one, who was probably old and the last in line. At least, that's the only way I can explain their luck. The poor fellow fell, and while the other rams vanished so quickly that not even the dogs could catch up with them, the hunters threw themselves upon him. What a disgusting spectacle it was. And for what? So that the important visitor could have a pelt and some horns. The horns were truly fine. 'He will brag about them for the rest of his life,' the interpreter said.

"It was this brutal murder," Turgen went on, "that awoke in me pity for the rams. I was more sly after that and led the party only to places when rams would never go. When the officials grew angry, complaining that I was a poor guide and that because of me they were disgraced before the foreigner, I answered: 'What can I do? Your shooting has frightened the animals away and they have run for perhaps a hundred miles.' They complained and threatened some more. Then they held a council to decide where they could find another guide. But the Yakuts told them that Turgen was the best in the whole region. The affair might have ended differently, but it got cold suddenly, there was a blizzard, and the important visitor left post haste for his own country. Of course, I rejoiced that the rams were now left in peace. But for several winters I did not see them. They had gone from here. In time, as you know, they returned. I saw them rarely. They came and vanished. Still I was happy to have them living again in my mountains." As they listened intently, Marfa and the children shared Turgen's fears and happiness. Now they understood his affection for the rams.

CHAPTER 8

B Y STEPPING ON TO A LEDGE OUTSIDE HIS door, Turgen on a clear day had a wonderful view of the valley below and the mountains above him. When he tired of watching the tiny figures of men and women scurrying about at the foot of his hill, he had only to turn his eyes upward to see a different and fascinating sight. For there, dodging among the crags, were specks which he knew to be wild rams.

"How do they live?" he asked himself one evening. The hills were barren except for sparse tufts of moss, an occasional thin clump of grass, and now and then a tough, hardy shrub that could not contain much nourishment.

His curiosity and pity aroused, Turgen watched the rams intently all that season and the next. He could make out nine individuals of what he assumed to be a family—or, as he called it, a tribe. In summer one lamb—or it might be

33

two—were added to the number, but they disappeared with cold weather.

Then Turgen began to worry. For with the cold weather came snow to cover the moss and grass and dry up the meager shrubs. Even at a distance he could sense the animals' despair as they searched avidly beneath the snow for any poor morsel to chew upon. Their gray-brown wool hung loosely on them now, and they moved indifferently, without spirit. Unless there was a hint of danger. Then they would lift their heads proudly and take themselves into the distance with incredible lightness and speed.

"Poor things." Turgen spoke his thoughts aloud. "To think that I used to hunt you to kill you! What harm are you to anyone? You who ask only for freedom."

But pity could not help them. He must find a way to give them practical aid. He considered one thing, then another. At last he fixed upon a plan.

First he built a light sleigh which he loaded with hay. Then, putting on skis, he pulled the sleigh to the ridge of the next mountain, dumped the hay, and returned home. Not a ram was in sight, but he could feel their inquisitive and fearful eyes upon him from behind the boulders farther up the hill.

From his own door he watched them approach the hay

warily, circle it and trample it, and stoop to nibble at it. They seemed to fear a trap. But when he went back to the spot the hay was gone. After that he took frequent offerings of food to them, and gradually the rams came to accept his gifts without hesitation. Although they never approached him when he visited the feeding ground, he caught glimpses of them in hiding, awaiting his coming. In order to gain their greater confidence, he made it a point never to carry a gun. He even gave up his habit of carrying an iron-tipped stick which helped him in climbing. For he knew that all animals fear the rod which gives forth noise and fire.

It was not easy to conquer the fear of these wild creatures. It needed patience as well as understanding. But Turgen had both. Season after season he gave them care and attention, and was rewarded by knowing that they accepted him and depended upon him even though they did not fully trust him. A time came when they no longer hid from him but stood watching from a safe distance as if to determine what sort of being this was from whom they received nothing but good. And he had another satisfaction. The food he gave them worked a miracle in their appearance. They were no longer the sad, dishevelled animals of former days.

His heart leaped for joy one day when he went to the feeding ground and discovered the entire ram family gathered in a group on a little mound near by.

"Eh!" Turgen declared with pleasure. "You are truly a good-looking band—strong and healthy. And you eat now as if you enjoyed it."

The rams eyed him gravely, with an expression that might have been gratitude on their long homely faces.

"Yes," they seemed to be saying. "Perhaps your pampered cattle down below would not thrive on this fare, but for savages like us it is nourishing. You see, we are not looking to put on fat, merely to survive."

With these friends, who had become like his own children, Turgen knew that he would never again be lonely as before.

CHAPTER 9

"A GOOD MAN GREETS EACH NEW DAY AS if it were a holiday." Turgen thought of this proverb upon waking every morning now, because it described exactly the way he felt. By becoming the protector of these defenseless animals, he had found a mission which used all the warmth of his lonely heart. He only regretted that the idea of feeding the rams had occurred to him so late. "But why waste time in regret?" he reflected. "Better rejoice that the idea came to me at last."

In order not to give the rams occasion for fright, it was necessary to change certain of his habits. For one thing, he did no hunting at all in the neighborhood of his yurta and the rams' feeding ground, but travelled some distance before permitting himself to fire a shot. He was gratified to discover before long that with the coming of spring birds and small animals, especially squirrels, flocked to his mountain side in great numbers. It was as if a rumor had spread that his place was their assurance of safety. The next spring and the next it was the same. Gay and charming visitors he had never known before came to delight him with their presence, and he felt himself being drawn into another world. How wonderful to be looked upon as a friend rather than as an enemy of these creatures!

In three years the rams, too, showed growing confidence in him. He fed them regularly, even when the snow melted and the crevices of the rocky hills revealed young grass and tender new shoots on the shrubs.

One sunny day he had gone as usual to the Rams' Mountain and was standing on a ledge near the feeding ground waiting for them to appear. Soon he saw three coming cautiously toward him. Quickly he stepped out of sight. By their watchful movements he judged that they had been sent to reconnoitre, and he was more sure of this a moment later when they bleated a piercing "Ma-a! Ma-a!"

He could not doubt that this was a signal to inform hidden companions that all was well, for the entire ram family now appeared, led by a huge powerful fellow who held his head with its sharp spiralling horns proudly. "What strength! What assurance!" Turgen thought, enchanted. The long beard and tail indicated that the leader ram was not young, but his legs were slender and built to endure. He had a reddish-brown coat flecked here and there with white. By his extraordinary size and confident attitude he impressed his authority on the herd.

When the leader after a brief survey had satisfied himself that there was no danger he spoke calmly to his charges. "Ma-a!" he said. Whereupon all the rams fell to eating.

Turgen counted them: six females and three males— with two lambs not more than three weeks old, which he had not seen before. Unlike the lambs he had noticed briefly in previous seasons, these were gay and frisky and seemed prepared to enjoy a long life. Two lambs to six females was not a large increase. Still they were promise of new generations. Turgen was overjoyed. Surely the smaller one must be a girl, the larger one a boy. He watched them drink greedily of their mother's milk, then pick at some grass only to reject it disdainfully and return to their mothers. Clearly they preferred milk to the food of grown-ups.

Turgen could not take his eyes from the rams, his wild mountaineers. In his imagination he saw this little family grown into a great herd.

CHAPTER 10

JUST THEN THE LEADER SOUNDED A SHARP WARN-
ing upon which the rams vanished. Turgen looked to
see what had frightened them, but could discover
nothing amiss. He listened, and heard a noise as of sifting
sand and gravel. Someone must be there. But who? Then
his attentive eyes caught sight of a bear stealthily creeping
toward the clearing. He was enormous.

By nature a bear was clumsy and sluggish, no match in
speed for the light-footed rams, but he had his own sure
method of hunting. He would search out the path by which
the rams traveled to get food and water, and there he
would lie in wait for them behind one of the cliffs. He
would wait for hours, patiently. Providing the wind was in
his favor, his scent did not betray him and the rams would
come unsuspectingly within reach. Then a pounce, a single
blow of his enormous paw, and the nearest ram would be
killed.

Turgen knew all this, knew also that the bear before him was an experienced hunter. Lacking a gun, he was powerless to give the rams any help. He thought of shouting, remembering that a bear is afraid of the human voice, but this might frighten the rams even more and decide them to seek another place of refuge. What then was he to do?

Rocks! He would throw rocks at the bear.

Taking quick aim, he fired a stone which lit near the bear's feet. The animal stopped, turned his head to sniff the air from all directions. When his eyes fixed upon Turgen above him, he let out a roar of fright that echoed from cliff to cliff and threw himself down the hillside. The clatter was terrific as he rolled over brush and outthrustings of rocks, crashing and bouncing and setting in motion a series of small landslides.

Attracted by the racket the old ram reappeared farther up the mountain and stood watching his enemy's progress with an expression of contentment.

Satisfied that the rams were safe, Turgen started home conscious that the leader was following him with his eyes. A dreadful thought assailed him: What if the rams associated him with the bear? What if their old suspicion of man were aroused and they left this region for another?

CHAPTER 11

THAT NIGHT TURGEN COULD SLEEP LITTLE, but tossed and turned in anxiety lest his charges desert him. For they had become necessary to him, perhaps more necessary than he to them. The next morning he rose early and hurried to the feeding ground with a generous supply of grass. Good or bad, he must know the truth.

His fears were promptly quieted when he saw the rams' fresh tracks in the clearing. As usual, he deposited the hay, then stood behind a rock to wait. But not for long. First to come were the scouts, then the leader. Then the family. In spite of their dirty-brown coats they were to him a lovely sight in their strength and grace and daring. The old leader was like a king arrayed in tatters, fully three feet in height and nearly six feet from tip to tip. The females, appropriately, were smaller, with almost straight horns, and held themselves with a kind of humility.

But it was the lambs to whom Turgen's heart went out. "The darlings!" he whispered.

Of course, the shy one who never ventured from her mother's side was a female, the gay prankish one a male. If in his play he dared approach the cliff, the old leader recalled him with a snort to his anxious parent.

"Eh! They are splendid children."

The rams seemed at home and at ease wandering about the clearing, and Turgen was reminded that it took more than a single fright to make them forsake their accustomed haunts. They were known to be stubbornly faithful to the place which provided them with food and shelter.

Turgen was starting down the mountain to return home when he noticed the leader ram circle the clearing excitedly, then with amazing lightness spring to the top of a rocky ledge where he had a good view of the mountain side. Sharply he surveyed the region, and sharply gave warning.

The warning was taken up by the other males, and promptly the females ranged themselves in a circle with their rumps together and their heads pointing out. The lambs, held within the circle, pushed against their elders inquisitively in an effort to get out, where were the other males.

As a general, the leader was magnificent. From a height of at least twenty-five feet he dropped easily to the clearing and again made a full swing around its center edge. On another signal from him the males took posts along the cliff and the herd froze in position, front legs braced, horns lowered, all facing the exposed slope.

"An astonishing battle formation!" Turgen said to himself in excitement and wonder. The rams were prepared to fight off an enemy. But who was the enemy? "Wolves?" Turgen wondered. He had heard of rams' exploits in battle, but never had he seen anything like this.

Intently he watched, and soon he saw three forest wolves approaching the clearing, enormous beasts made bold and dangerous by hunger through the winter. His heart beat fast with terror for his herd. What he would have given for a gun! Lacking that, he made sure that his knife was ready to hand, even though he knew himself to be a helpless onlooker should the wolves attack. "For I'm not a bird and not a ram, to go from crag to crag," he thought.

The first wolf had reached the edge of the clearing now. With his mouth open, revealing powerful tusks, and the hair erect on his spine, he was terrifying to look at. Turgen heard him growl, a low fierce rumble, and waited for him

to pounce, but instead he flung himself full length on the ground while still keeping his burning eyes on the rams. Was he perhaps selecting his prey? Turgen did not know, but he saw how the female rams drew together in a closer circle behind the leader. It was quite clear by their staunch attitudes that the rams had no intention of running away.

What a battle it would be! But what chance had the rams against those three beasts?

The first wolf, tiring of inactivity and prompted by greed, decided against waiting longer for his companions and rose to his feet. Slowly he advanced. With each cautious step Turgen expected him to plunge.

Then an amazing thing happened. The old ram without warning, lowered his head to the ground and sprang at the advancing enemy. So exactly had he gauged the distance that his horns struck the wolf in the chest with an impact strong enough to raise him in the air and send him hurtling over the cliff. His howls echoed around the mountain as he fell and so distracted the other two wolves that they turned from the clearing and raced after their unlucky comrade.

It seemed not more than a minute that it took to wage and win the battle. Then the herd of rams broke formation to lie down and rest. Except for the lambs who were as full of play as ever.

Turgen, making his way home on legs which did not seem to belong to him, lived over again the old ram's victory. It was as if the triumph were his own.

CHAPTER 12

AT HOME HE COULD NOT GET THE INCIDENT out of his mind. These wild mountaineers had become like his own flesh and blood—what happened to them was his experience also.

It was midnight, but he could not sleep from excitement. Reaching for his reed, he started to play—and soon the yurta was filled with music that spoke of sadness and at the same time of quiet rejoicing. The melodies were new to him. They had seemingly sprung out of the air in order to celebrate the afternoon's wonderful adventure.

At last he lay down to rest. With all his heart he desired this night to see a fine dream. What kind of a dream he did not know, but he felt that he must communicate the day's fortune to the good spirit of the yurta. For had not a good spirit come to drive out the evil spirit when he made himself the protector of the rams? Turgen believed that it had. For his faith in God—the Great Spirit who ruled the world—did not exclude the possibility that there were other spirits known to his forefathers who acted as messengers for God and Satan and had more time to concern themselves with the affairs of a poor Lamut.

His wish was granted him. In his sleep he saw a joyous dream.

His wife and son entered the yurta, looking just as he remembered them. He wanted to welcome them, to say a thousand things he had in his mind to tell them, but no words came. He could only gaze at their dear faces in silent astonishment.

His wife came near, took him by the hand, smiled and said: "Turgen, get up and come with us. The Great Spirit is happy that you are taking care of the wild rams and wants to thank you personally."

Turgen rose as he was directed and went with them. But his wife and son seemed to float through the air rather than walk and he had great difficulty keeping up. Up hills, over vertical cliffs he followed after them, gasping from exhaustion and fearful that they would abandon him.

Finally he called out in despair: "Help me. I cannot keep up with you. If you do not help me, I shall never see the Great Spirit."

Encouragingly his wife answered: "Yes, Turgen, you are tired. But don't be afraid. We will help you."

With that she took him by one hand, the son by the other, and all three rose into the air. Higher and higher they flew, to dizzy heights where it was hard to breathe, and came at last to a mountain whose top was lost in the clouds. When they had landed in a small field Turgen looked around him amazed.

"What an immense place!" he exclaimed. "If the Great Spirit lives this far away it is no wonder that we never see him."

The place was remarkable for more than its size. The mountains familiar to Turgen were also high, but bleak and bare. Here were fields with trees and flowers growing in abundance and giving off odors that tickled the nostrils. And in the midst of the wonders he saw lambs browsing under the guardianship of wolves.

"What is this?" he asked his wife. "How can such young things be entrusted to killer-beasts?"

Smilingly she said: "There are no killers here, Turgen. Here everyone—birds, animals, people—live in love and harmony."

"Wonderful!" Turgen exclaimed. "I should like to live here myself for a while."

"You will in due time," the woman assured him. "But come now—the Great Spirit is expecting you."

Turgen looked around, expecting to see a large yurta in which the Great Spirit lived, but instead he saw only a great larch tree and under it a bench very like his own. An aged man dressed in white was sitting there, a man who bore striking resemblance to his long-dead grandfather.

"Who is this?" Turgen asked himself. "Is it possible that he is the Great Spirit? I did not picture him so. This man is lean and not very tall and there is nothing of grandeur about him. No doubt he is a servant."

But meeting the old man's eyes, which held a kind of fire, he was seized with fear and reverence. Humbly he fell on his knees and whispered: "Forgive me, Almighty! I, a sinner, failed to recognize you. How could I recognize you, since I have never seen you?"

A gentle voice replied: "Rise, my son. Do not be afraid. If you have not seen me, yet you heard me when I said to you, 'Turgen, go feed the starving rams. They are my children too, just as you are.' Your heart is open to goodness. You have given me much joy. Now rise and sit here beside me."

Eagerly, Turgen leaped to his feet—and woke up.

CHAPTER 13

FOR A MOMENT HE WAS GRIEVOUSLY DISAP-pointed at having lost his dream, but soon a great happiness overtook him. Surely this was no ordinary dream, he told himself. The Great Spirit in his mysterious wisdom had chosen this way to make his favor known. Although Turgen longed to rush down the hill and share the night's adventure with Marfa and her children, he didn't—because the dream, for a reason he was at a loss to explain, seemed to belong to him alone.

Did Marfa notice that something of extraordinary importance had happened to him? If so, she gave no sign, for it was not her habit to question. Nevertheless, Turgen felt a sense of guilt that he should conceal anything from his kind friends.

The children especially might well have asked: "Turgen, why don't you tell us stories any more? Why don't you play the reed and sit by the komelek and smoke?"

For he did none of these things, being so preoccupied by his own thoughts and concerns. He went for his milk as usual, gave abrupt greetings, asked absurd quetions which deserved no answers, and quickly departed.

The truth was, he had to admit honestly, that the family of rams had become dearer to him than anything or anyone.

At home there was more than enough work to keep him busy, for it was important that he make good use of what was left of the summer. Hay must be dried and stored for the rams, wood chopped to last a long winter, fish and game caught and packed away in a small cellar not far from the yurta—a hole dug in the ground where food stayed fresh summer and winter. He remembered the old proverb:

"What the summer gives, the winter will swallow."

As a result of his dream he suddenly gave most careful attention to his housekeeping. Every day he swept the floor, and he polished the kettles and pots until they shone. He did this because, secretly, he cherished the hope that his wife and son would visit him again. Maybe—who knows?—the Great Spirit himself might condescend to drop in.

But always the rams came first. At least twice a week, in

every kind of weather, he carried food to them. He fed them even though the mountains were still green with vegetation, because they were now more than ever necessary to him. Besides, the succulent grass which he gathered in the valley gave variety to their diet and they loved it. While the rams never came close to him but maintained a respectful distance, they showed no nervousness at sight of him, and this pleased him very much.

The summer, brief as a dream, had brought changes in the flock. The rams had taken on flesh, their coats were soft and thick and of a uniform brown except for tufts of white on the sides, under the groin and neck. The similar markings confirmed Turgen's belief that they were of the same family. Warm weather and plenty of food had made them active, also; often, out of sheer high spirits, two grown up males would lock horns in combat. And every day, it seemed, the lambs were inspired to new feats of inventiveness and daring.

The male lamb especially enchanted Turgen. Everything his elders did he tried to imitate, executing leaps that made Turgen's heart turn over in fear. At times his impudent pranks brought him a sharp reprimand from the leader.

"The scamp!" Turgen exclaimed. "That one was born to get himself noticed."

Soon, Turgen reminded himself, he must exercise still greater vigilance for with autumn hunters would be abroad in the hills. While he doubted that his superstitious neighbors from the valley would come near his yurta, stranger things had happened and he dared not count on it. To every hunter the rams were an irresistible attraction.

CHAPTER 14

SEPTEMBER CAME, BRINGING ITS CUSTOMARY changeable weather. One damp and windy day when all the furies seemed loose, Turgen went as usual to take food to his charges and stand watch.

"Though why anyone should come out in this weather I don't know," he thought. "Even the rams will surely keep under shelter."

But no. He had time only to drop the hay and retreat to his watching post when they were in full strength—the whole family. The rain annoyed them and they shook themselves from time to time. Otherwise they showed no discomfiture. While the leader and two other males circled the clearing on the alert for danger, the rest stood quietly in the lee of the cliff waiting for the rain to abate. Looking for the lambs, Turgen saw them lying snugly under their mothers' bellies.

At the first sign of the weather's clearing Turgen's favorite jumped up and ran to urge the second lamb to romp with him. She refused, preferring her comfort. He then advanced on the older rams, trying by all the wiles he could command to get their attention. Turgen almost laughed aloud watching his antics.

"What a show-off!" Then he worried. "It is cold and wet for one so young. He will get sick.—But that's an absurd idea. He is not made of clay that he will melt."

Soon after this the rain stopped and Turgen started for home. He had gone only a few steps when a shot rang out. There were hunters somewhere in the hills nearby—too far away to menace the herd of rams but the sound of gunfire alone was enough to cause panic. While the echo was still curling around the mountains the rams crowded around the leader as he stood irresolute, his head raised, his nostrils distended to test the air. It was he who must say what they should do.

In a minute the old ram turned and came at a light trot across a narrow stone abutment that formed a natural bridge between the clearing and the adjoining hill where Turgen stood. Without hesitation the other rams followed him in single file, males and females alternating. Turgen's lamb was behind his mother and just in front of the male ram who brought up the rear. The bridge led to a labyrinth of caves where escape was easy. That it led past Turgen seemed a matter of no concern to the rams in the face of great danger.

The bridge was no doubt slippery but the rams were sure-footed and they did not give way to panic. They were moving in a direction away from the gunfire. But Turgen had another plan. He would go toward the place from which the shot came. Should he meet the hunter, the hunter would understand that he was trespassing and leave the neighborhood—for such was the custom. Only one hunter was allowed to a region.

But before Turgen could act on his resolve, there was another shot. The ram at the end of the line, hearing it, jumped, made an incautious step, and knocked against the lamb, who fell from the bridge.

CHAPTER 15

TURGEN'S HEART TURNED IN HIM AS HE watched the small body hurtle down the crevasse. Then, peering over, he saw the lamb lying motionless on the mountain slope. Quickly, he made his way to the spot, fearing that wild animals would get there first.

The lamb's eyes, raised to his, were black with terror. It tried convulsively to rise but could not.

"Thank God, he's alive," was Turgen's first thought. "There's a chance I can save him."

With that he stooped and lifted the lamb gently.

"Ma-a," said the lamb in a weak, childish whimper. And from a distance came a mournful answering bleat. "Ma-a! Ma-a!" that might have been the old leader. Then fog enveloped the mountain.

The lamb was surprisingly heavy, but Turgen hardly noticed the burden in his anxiety and excitement. Carefully he made his way to the yurta through the darkness, and as he went he murmured reassurance to his patient, who made no further effort to escape.

"It is not far to go. Be quiet. Rest. Do not fear—I'll do you no harm." Over and over Turgen said it, like a chant.

At the yurta Turgen laid the lamb on some soft pelts to examine him. Noticing fresh blood stains, he looked for a wound and found a flesh cut under the right front leg. It took but a minute to wash it clean and cover it with a poultice of plantain leaves to stop the bleeding.

The lamb's fright returned now and he struggled to gain his feet. But his hind legs would not obey him.

"There, there, lad," Turgen soothed him with tender strokes and pats. "What are you afraid of? I will soon make you well and take you back to your family. Who am I but an old man? There is no harm in me. Besides, who would dare to lift a hand against such a splendid fellow? Lie still. Trust me."

Pain, weariness, and the strange but unterrifying sound made by a human voice finally had their effect. The lamb rested while Turgen explored more thoroughly for possible injuries. There were scratches and bruises, none of them serious. And one hind leg was plainly swollen.

"God forbid that it should be broken," Turgen thought

in dismay. For he was expert with animals and he knew the difficulty of keeping a wild young thing quiet while bone mended.

Fortunately, he found that the injury was no more than a dislocation, but extremely painful to the touch. With practiced skill, while the patient bleated piteously, he swathed the whole body to keep it immobile except for the head. Then, quickly and deftly, he set the bone, bandaged the leg and hoof between splints and satisfied himself that the lamb could do no harm to the injury should he get on his feet. As he worked the lamb regarded him with fixed and startled eyes. It was breathing heavily and clearly would have liked to offer resistance.

The bandaging operation finished, the lamb grew calm, fright gave way to weariness.

"Why," Turgen thought. "There is the same look in his eyes that I saw in Tim's when I set his arm. Children are alike. They suffer more from fright than pain." To the lamb he said: "That other little fellow drank some milk and fell asleep when I had doctored him. And so should you."

Fortunately, Turgen had only the day before brought milk from Marfa's cow. It stood untouched in the cellar. He poured some into a large wooden bowl and offered it to the lamb. At first the lamb turned his head away in distaste, but when by accident a few drops found their way into his mouth he smacked his lips with enjoyment. After that he drank willingly, with relish, looking at Turgen as if to say: "Really, this isn't bad at all."

Turgen was beside himself with joy as his charge finished his meal and promptly went to sleep.

"Food and attention—that's all anyone wants," Turgen reflected. "Just food and attention."

It was late when he himself was ready for bed, and after the agitating events of the day he slept fitfully. Whenever he wakened, as he did frequently, his first thought was for the lamb—and this stranger in his yurta seemed not a wild ram but a person close and dear to him. By going to his rescue, Turgen had found someone to share his yurta.

It is true, he marvelled, what our people say: "Misfortune can sometimes bring happiness."

CHAPTER 16

MAN IS A CHANGEABLE CREATURE—DESPAIR-ing one moment, filled with joy and confidence the next. "The sun shines differently every day," was the way Turgen's father had put it, and he found wisdom in the words. How different yesterday was from today, he thought upon wakening, and all because of two dark eyes full of anxiety which greeted him across the room.

Turgen rose, went to the lamb and stroked its head, under the soft brown-gray curls were hard knob-like growths which would one day become horns. Although the lamb shrank from his touch and tried to hide by closing its eyes, it did not struggle as before. Nor did fear prevent it from drinking a large bowl of milk for breakfast.

"Oho!" Turgen exclaimed with satisfaction. "Anyone with a hearty appetite like yours can not be suffering from internal injuries."

After the feeding, Turgen washed his patient's wounds and covered them with a mixture of fish oil and tar. "The oil is healing, the smell of tar will keep flies and insects away." This, too, Turgen had learned from his father. He thought of freeing the lamb of the bandages, but decided "No. He's too young and frightened to be trusted. He would only injure himself more." As he worked Turgen talked aloud, sometimes to himself and sometimes to the lamb but always keeping his voice quiet so that the young stranger would not take alarm.

The chores that day were like child's play, so busy was Turgen's mind with plans. Returning from Marfa's with a fresh supply of milk for Lad, as he called the lamb—he thought, "What good fortune has come to me. When Lad gets well I will take him back to the herd myself." And he pictured the reunion of the rams, how Lad would tell his family of Turgen's kindness. Who could say?—the news might even reach the ears of the Great Spirit. For Turgen could not forget his dream. He was convinced the lamb had come to him for a purpose, as a messenger from the old man on the mountain to test Turgen's devotion. Should he receive care and attention, then Turgen at his death would be granted permission to enter that world of beauty where his wife and son dwelt, where wolves were nurses to creatures supposed to be their natural enemies.

Such thoughts made Turgen very happy. It seemed that on this bright and sparkling day the birds were gayer, the grass greener, the brook more talkative than he had ever known them to be before.

When Lad's wants had been attended to, Turgen went as usual to the Rams' Mountain with a feeding of hay. To his disappointment no rams appeared, though he waited behind his special rock for some time.

"Is it possible they have gone away because of yesterday's accident?" he worried. "No, surely not. They will return. They must. Not just because of the food, but to look for the lamb."

This thought had hardly come to him when he caught sight of the leader ram opposite him on the stone bridge. The old fellow moved slowly, stopping from time to time to peer into the ravine. There was something very forlorn about him and Turgen's heart went out to him. As he came to the middle of the bridge he paused, then on what seemed to be a sudden impulse, he turned, leaped and vanished.

Had he gone back to the herd? Turgen wondered. But no. There he was on the ledge where the lamb had fallen.

"Eh, poor fellow," Turgen addressed him silently. "It's too bad I can't tell you that your boy is alive, that I am caring for him and will soon return him to you. Don't grieve. I will keep my word. And you—you must not go away from here."

CHAPTER 17

URGEN HAD BUT ONE DETERMINATION—TO see the lamb well again and back with his family.

The first few days were difficult. Although Lad was not as fearful and suspicious as before, he was restive and tried by every trick to free himself of the bandages. At the first opportunity, when the shoulder wound began to heal, Turgen removed the wrappings.

Like a flash, Lad sprang to his feet, shook himself, stretched, and bounded onto Turgen's bed. Then a look of astonishment came into his eyes as he noticed his wooden leg. After gazing around the yurta he turned to Turgen as if to question him.

"Where am I? Who are you? Why do you live in such a tiny cave, where there is no room for leaping? And why is my leg so stiff?"

Turgen would have sworn that these were the questions in Lad's eyes. As he filled a bowl with milk he answered softly. "You are surprised, but don't be afraid, boy. That drone, maybe your brother or uncle, who was behind you pushed you off the cliff. Remember? You have hurt yourself. But in a couple of weeks you will be quite well again. Believe me."

Lad accepted attention willingly now. He ate and drank with an appetite and submitted with evident enjoyment to being petted. But Turgen knew that he was not to be trusted too far, so he made a collar and leash when he wanted to take the lamb out for exercise.

Upon leaving the yurta for the first time Lad stopped as if thunderstruck by the sunlight and the sight of his familiar mountains. Intoxicated with delight and longing, he plunged forward but the leash held him fast. He turned, called in a piercing voice—"Ma-a, Ma-a . . ." Then, receiving no answer, he jumped and circled desperately in an effort to be free.

"Come, come," said Turgen as he picked up the young savage and carried him back to the yurta. "I understand that you are reminded of your home and family. You are tired of this dark cage and impatient to be gone. But there are things that can't be rushed. Calm yourself."

So for the next two days Lad stayed in the yurta while Turgen devoted himself to his comfort and was entertained in turn. The lamb learned to take his milk with a mixture of barley meal and water. He learned that grass was good to eat, and how to distinguish the sweet, tender blades from the tough dry ones which pricked and gave no satisfaction. Turgen never tired of watching him. To his fond eyes Lad was beautiful with his proud little head so like the leader ram's and soft coat of dark brown spotted with white near groin and haunches. A darker streak the length of his long face from forehead to nostrils gave him the expression of a solemn clown.

"Truly, you are a handsome lad," Turgen assured him.

Lad loved praise, and did not question anything Turgen told him. Free to go where he pleased indoors, he tapped his way boldly about the yurta, thrusting his nose into everything, sniffing, examining like a curious puppy. Only once did he show fright, when a fir log suddenly sputtered in the komelek and sent out a shower of sparks. After that he treated the fire with mixed caution and respect.

Yes, Turgen thought, this four-legged wild creature had made his life over and filled it with a great content.

CHAPTER 18

I T WAS SEVERAL DAYS BEFORE TURGEN FOUND
time to return to the feeding ground with hay for the
rams. It troubled him that he had neglected them,
but in honesty he had to admit that with Lad for company
he did not think so often of the others. He wondered
whether he would miss them greatly should they abandon
their mountain—providing, of course, they left Lad behind.

"But that is a dreadful thought," he reproached himself
the next instant. "How could I take advantage of them by
robbing them of their young one? No, no, I will return him
to his family."

It crossed his mind also that the Great Spirit would be
angry if he betrayed his trust.

Again the only ram he could see was the leader standing
on a rocky ledge above him. Turgen imagined that the old
fellow was questioning him as their glances met. Impulsively he shouted: "It's all right, my friend. The lad is doing

well and I will bring him back to you myself in a couple of weeks."

To his pleasure the ram did not shy from his voice but seemed to wait for further news of the lost one.

"He knows me. He knows me, and he is not afraid," Turgen gloated. The rams would stay now, he was sure.

Returning home, he was still some distance from the yurta when he heard Lad calling "Ma-a! Ma-a!" Just inside the door the lamb was waiting with eyes which said accusingly, "You stayed away a long time. Why? I'm lonesome and I'm hungry."

Not a movement escaped the sharp young eyes as Turgen busied himself preparing food, and everywhere Turgen went Lad came clumping behind him. There was no doubt he had been alarmed by Turgen's absence and welcomed him home.

"Eh, my darling, you are very clever," Turgen complimented him. And to test him further he called the little savage by name: "Lad, Lad."

Lad cocked his head attentively, which was the only sign Turgen needed that they understood each other well.

A few days later Turgen examined the lamb's injuries to satisfy himself that the dislocation was mending properly and there was no infection, but it was a week or more before he decided that it was safe to remove the splints. Lad was at first bewildered, then surprised, then delighted. He leaped on the bed and down again. He pranced and pirouetted. But when Turgen later took him for a walk he showed no desire to run away. He was happy with the day which was as perfect as September sometimes brings to the Far North. He was happy with the limited freedom he was permitted on the end of his leash. Joyously he danced and flung himself into the air, lowered his head to the ground and kicked his legs high. And when he had had his fill he came to Turgen of his own accord singing "Ma-a, Ma-a . . ." in a voice warm with contentment.

Gladly this time he followed Turgen back to the yurta, and entered as if the place belonged to him. A little later, having finished a hearty meal, he folded his legs under him and fell sound asleep. Just like any healthy infant, thought Turgen with pride.

CHAPTER 19

R EASONING THAT A CHILD CAN TELL YOU
when he is in pain and where the pain is, but an
animal can not, Turgen watched intently to make
sure that Lad ate and drank as he should and regularly
fulfilled the demands of nature. By this time he was fully
assured that the lamb did not suffer internal injuries. It
was a pleasant duty Turgen performed, making certain that
this wild young thing survived its mishap, and when
occasionally he saw the old ram scrutinizing him inquisitively from the mountainside he thought that the Great
Spirit himself might be keeping just as watchful an eye on
him. "To see that I carry out His wishes."

Does it seem strange that the old ram and the Great
Spirit of Turgen's dream appeared to him sometimes as
one and the same person? It was not strange to Turgen,
who believed quite simply that the Great Spirit was everywhere at all times. "Only man is too busy during the day

to visit with Him. Therefore He comes at night to call bringing new faith and strength." Surely He was powerful enough to take the shape of a ram if He so desired.

Such thoughts comforted Turgen and softened his dread of having to part with Lad.

With freedom to move about, young Lad joyfully took over the yurta. Each day he became more attached to Turgen, following at his heels like a dog as he went about his chores. The clearing outside the yurta he also considered to be his special province and he made no move to run away even when he was once allowed to go without collar or leash.

His eyes questioned sometimes when the day was clear and the breeze fresh off the hills: "Tell me—what of my family?" And at such times Turgen answered: "They are well, believe me. And you are remembered. I see the old ram often. When you return you must assure him that I was good to you." When Lad shook his head, pirouetted and leaped for glee, Turgen took his antics to mean: "Ay— I certainly will."

It was one day when Lad was frolicking in the clearing and dancing on his hind legs that the drunkard Nikita happened along and saw him. Mistaking the lamb for the devil, Nikita fled shouting down the mountain while Lad, equally alarmed by the strange voice, rushed to Turgen for protection.

Turgen guessed the cause of Nikita's terror. "What a fool!" he remarked to the flying figure. "Now he will spread more lies about me. But what can one do? To shoot at a rock is but a waste of arrows."

That same evening Marfa reported the excitement in the valley when Nikita spread the news of what he had seen. "He was like a madman," she said sharply, "shouting that he saw you at play with the devil and the devil must be killed. When I noticed people listening to him, I gave them a piece of my mind. I told them what they already knew if their heads were not stuffed with hay—that there isn't a better man among them than you. No, nor a better hunter or fisherman. They are envious—that is all. So they believe an idler whose words are worth nothing. With his drunken eyes he saw a wild ram. Tphoo! Of course he lied."

Tim and Aksa looked at their mother in amazement. This was not the gentle woman they knew.

Turgen shook his head regretfully. "Thank you, Marfa, but you shouldn't fret yourself so. Remember that dry mud won't stick to a wall. And to listen to gossip is like bailing out water with a sieve. It is true that Nikita saw a wild ram lamb with me. Not a full grown ram but a lamb which fell from a cliff and was injured. Since I have been caring for him he has become almost tame. That is all. There is no sorcery about it. Perhaps I should have told you. But as you know, I am not much of a talker."

Tim and Aksa listened, their eyes burning with curiosity and excitement. They were afraid to ask questions before their mother's anger had cooled.

Marfa herself was surprised by what Turgen told her, but after a moment's thought she declared vehemently, "Well, what's so remarkable about your caring for a poor little lamb? The fools might better wonder at your kindness and your skill than spread these silly stories. And I shall tell them so."

Marfa shook her fist as warning to those "dumb ones." Then to the children's delight she asked Turgen to stay for a cup of tea. Now they would hear more about Turgen's surprising guest. A mountain lamb! Surely this was the finest of all possible treasures. But to their disappointment Turgen was not in a mood to talk, and in fear of their mother they held their itching tongues.

CHAPTER 20

WALKING HOME THAT EVENING, TURGEN was troubled as he thought over what Marfa had told him.

"Such silly tattle can do me no harm," he reasoned, "but what if someone takes it into his stupid head to sneak up the hill and shoot Lad? So long as he stays with me there will be this danger. I must give him back to his family as quickly as possible. There in the mountains he will have protection."

The resolution did not make him happy, especially when he saw how Lad welcomed him and clung to him.

"How strange," Turgen thought, "that a wild animal can understand affection while people, who should be wiser, can not."

For a long time he could not fall asleep but tossed from side to side thinking of the empty days ahead when he would be alone again. Weariness finally won, however, just as he was praying: "Great Spirit, have pity on me . . . help me . . . teach me."

Then Turgen dreamed. In his dream it was raining and there were loud crashes of thunder following upon lightning. He went out of the yurta just in time to see the Great Spirit rush past. But so swift was his flight that Turgen had no time to utter a word. Bitterly disappointed, he returned indoors, thinking, "Evidently I am unworthy to talk to Him."

But hardly had he lain down again when someone knocked on the door.

"Come in, come in," Turgen called, and the door opened to admit a gray-haired old man who looked strangely like himself. He carried a staff in his hand and a pack on his back.

The visitor bowed, saying, "Thank you, Turgen, for your invitation. It is raining and I am tired. You live so far from me."

Turgen, delighted to have company, begged his guest, "Come, sit closer to the fire, friend, and rest yourself. I will get you something to eat." Then, struck by the old man's appearance, he added: "Why do you climb mountains in this weather at your age? You're not strong enough for that. You see my yurta—it is spacious and I live here alone, except for this lamb. But I must return him soon to his family. Won't you stay and make your home with me?"

It didn't surprise Turgen that Lad awoke just then, jumped from his corner, and going over to the visitor placed his head on the old man's knees. The visitor stroked him as he said, "You are a good boy and you fell into the hands of a good man."

Turgen, rejoicing at such praise, replied: "The lamb and his family are a worry to me because people hunt them, even though they are harmless. It is my belief that they should be allowed to live in freedom and peace like . . ." He was about to say, "like the birds and beasts who dwell with the Great Spirit," but something told him that his guest already knew what was in his mind for he was nodding. "There is a whole tribe of wild rams not far from here," Turgen went on. "Splendid animals. While I am alive I'll see that no one molests them. But I am old and alone. Who will look after them when I die?"

Instead of giving him the sympathy he expected, the old man burst out in anger: "Alone, alone! And whose fault is that? Your own. Happiness is right under your nose, but you don't see it. You are blind as a bat! Why don't you ask Marfa and her children to share your yurta with you? She is a fine woman, and so are the children."

"You know," Turgen replied, taken aback, "I never thought of that. But it is not yet too late."

"Don't wait too long," the visitor advised him. "Inquire of your heart and act as it prompts you. In such matters the heart is better than the head."

Turgen started to say that he agreed but would have to consult Marfa—and what would the Yakuts say who called him a sorcerer?

But the old man answered him before he could speak: "Don't let this disturb you. Marfa and the children will be delighted. As for the Yakuts—don't pay any attention to them. It is not that they are evil, only ignorant. Believe me."

At this moment, before he could thank the visitor for his advice, Turgen awoke. So real was his dream that he could not rid himself of it. "Amazing," he murmured. "A miracle."

The yurta was quiet. The fire in the komelek was dying. The lamb slept peacefully in his corner.

Being a man of simple faith, Turgen did not doubt that the dream was a sign given him by unknown powers. Had he wanted to ask Marfa before to bring the children and share his yurta? If so, he would never have found the courage alone to speak to her of his desire. The dream made everything simple and right. He had begged the

Great Spirit for help, and help was given him in the form of advice. Now he had only to act.

It was Lad who roused Turgen from his reflections by butting him gently and crying, "Ma-a, Ma-a . . ."

"Yes, yes," he agreed. "It is nearly daylight and time to get up and you are hungry. Come, we'll have breakfast and off we'll go."

Although it was the last meal they would have together, Turgen was not sad. Two thoughts were uppermost in his mind: Lad was going back to his family where he belonged, and Turgen would soon have a family of his own to love and care for.

CHAPTER 21

RESOLUTELY TURGEN SET OFF FOR THE FEED-
ing ground with a bundle of hay slung over his
shoulder and the lamb skipping along by his
side. They might have been out for one of their usual
walks. But as they approached the clearing Turgen noted
how the lamb hesitated and looked about him expectantly.

"Something tells him that he has been in this place
before," thought Turgen. The thought made him happy
and filled with inner peace . . .

Suddenly Lad turned sharply and sang out in his youthful
voice—"Ma-a, Ma-a."

In reply came the same call, but more strongly and
Turgen, searching the cliffs, saw the old ram standing in
his full magnificence as if frozen to the rocky promontory.
There was amazement in the look he directed at the man
and the returned lamb.

Turgen shouted: "Come, old man. Come here and accept

your son. You see, I did bring him back to you. As you can see, he is well and happy."

In answer, the ram raised his head and sent a bellow—"Ma-a, ma-a"—echoing around the hills. Joy, surprise, and anxiety were in his voice, Turgen understood. For how could this savage be expected to trust his old enemy man?

While the ram stood there irresolute, not quite able to believe his eyes, Lad whirled in a frenzy of excitement and started toward the cliff. Memory guided him and he ran along the same stone bridge from which he had fallen. But Turgen had no fear for him now. "Take care of yourself, Lad," he called. "Good-bye, my dear!"

Upon hearing his voice the lamb stopped briefly to send back an affectionate—"Ma-a, ma-a." It was both "Good-bye" and "Thank you." With that he disappeared around a bend.

For a moment both rams were lost to view. Then they reappeared on the cliff together—the old fellow and the youngster who was so like him.

Turgen greeted them joyfully: "I can see that you are glad to have Lad back and safe. He will tell you that people are not all evil."

The rams answered him in soft chorus, and vanished. But they would return—again and again. Of that Turgen was certain. There was a pact between them now that could not be broken. Turgen would feed the family and protect them from hunters. The old ram, so wise and strong, would guard the herd against other enemies such as wolves and bears.

"Until some day Lad grows up and takes his place as leader," Turgen promised. He was confident that he could foretell this much of the future.

CHAPTER 22

TURGEN HAD KNOWN MARFA AS A FRIEND FOR many years, but it had never entered his head to suggest that she and her children share his life. Now here he was on his way to her, his mind filled with this very idea. Yet the nearer he came to her yurta the more absurd he appeared to himself. He was tortured with doubts.

What was a man of his age to say to her? "Look Marfa— I live alone, make my own fires, do my own cooking and sewing, and worry about no one but myself. It's not natural. So I have come to ask you to be my wife."

Certainly a sensible woman like Marfa could only say, "Why, you old fogey, are you out of your senses? What would the neighbors think if I went to live with you, whom they consider a sorcerer?"

Such thoughts made Turgen's legs grow cold and his feet

drag. Still, he reminded himself, he was following a dream. The Great Spirit had spoken to him, and he believed.

Nothing was as he imagined it. Perhaps it was that heart spoke to heart. At any rate, the moment he entered the yurta, Marfa gave one glance at him and exclaimed:

"Turgen, your face shines like a nicely polished copper kettle! Something wonderful must have happened to you! Is that true? Tell me."

Turgen thought, "How could I have doubted my dream? I did not know how to speak and she has prompted me. But I'll lead up to the question gradually."

To Marfa he said: "You see, today I returned Lad to his family. I fulfilled the promise made to the Great Spirit. It was good, don't you think?"

"Yes," Marfa answered, perplexed, "but why are you so happy? I thought you were very much attached to him. And now you'll be alone again."

"Yes, Marfa, but listen. I rejoice because the wild rams are my own. I have had a sign. They will stay and I will look after them. Don't you understand that the Great Spirit himself has talked to me and thanked me?"

"Wait, wait, Turgen," Marfa interrupted. "I don't understand a word of what you're saying. I believe in the good spirits, but I can't say that I have ever talked with them.

I've never even seen them in a dream. Are you sure you are in your right mind?" There was anxiety in her voice.

Turgen smiled as he said firmly, "I am not out of my mind. Listen to this—" And he told her from beginning to end how he had become interested in the starving rams, how he had tended them and saved the lamb. He told her too about his marvelous dreams. It seemed to him that never before in his life had he been so eloquent.

Toward the end, looking at Marfa's attentive, smiling face, Turgen knew without doubt that she understood everything he would say.

When he had finished she put her hand on his head affectionately as if he were one of her children and said: "You are a good man, Turgen . . . And your dreams are good, too. I wish nothing better for myself or for the children. I know that they love you. We will all be happy. And once we are living as husband and wife, people will stop their evil gossip."

She turned to Tim and Aksa, who were listening with curiosity and whispering to each other. "Children, Turgen will live with us from now on. Are you glad?"

"Yes, yes!" they answered, their voices eager, their eyes sparkling. They were delighted.

CHAPTER 23

THAT WAS A DAY OF GAIETY AND LAUGHTER for all of them. When Turgen left toward evening, Aksa who was more talkative and more inquisitive than her brother asked her mother,

"Now that Turgen belongs to us, will we go to live in his yurta?"

"No, daughter," Marfa replied. "We will live here, for he has not enough room for us, and up in the mountains there is no food for a cow. In the summer we can visit him."

This did not entirely please the children, who hoped that their new life would be full of change and excitement. To live in the mountains, which they did not know except from the valley, would be wonderful. But grown-ups could not be expected to understand.

"I want to look at the sky from the top of a mountain," Aksa declared. "Turgen says that good children can see angels in the sky. But I would be happy just to see their wings."

Tim spoke up firmly: "And I want to see Lad and the other rams."

"So do I," Aksa added quickly, not to be left out.

Marfa smiled. "Turgen is coming again early tomorrow morning, and if you ask him he might take you home with him for a visit. If the weather is warm you can even stay over night."

"Oh, Mama!" the children exclaimed. "Will you ask him, too?"

"Of course."

That night the children prayed that the next day would be warm and Turgen would accept them as his guests, so it did not surprise them upon wakening to find the day bright and their friend bending over them.

"Dress yourselves, children," Turgen said, smiling, "I am very glad to take you with me if you think you can stand the walk uphill."

"Oh, we can. We are good walkers," they answered him.

Soon they were ready for what was their first adventure away from home. Marfa gave them milk to take along, with barley cakes and dried fish.

A twisted path led up the mountain. Turgen walked in

front, with Aksa behind him, and Tim bringing up the rear. The path followed a talkative little brook and all around was heavy shrubbery with tall fir trees, larches, and graceful white birches for background. Their progress was slow because the children must stop every few steps to pick and eat some of the black and red currants and bird-cherry berries so tasty this time of year.

Birds overhead twittered so noisily that Aksa asked Turgen seriously, "What do you think? Are they rejoicing because we are here?"

"I wouldn't be surprised," he answered just as seriously. "It is well known that birds like good children."

Everything amazed the children. The familiar brook was brighter, swifter, more mysterious in this higher ground. The woods held fascinations and terrors they could only imagine. Never having been far away from their yurta in the valley, they were—thanks to Turgen—entering a brand-new world. If they stopped frequently, it was not only because of the berries or because they were tired, but because they needed time to take in all the wonders. From up here the valley was a different place than they had known—like a child's plaything laid out in squares of green and brown, with the brook wending through it, a silver thread.

"How close it is!" they marveled. "And we thought we had walked a long way. Close and small."

"Yes," Turgen said, as they strained their eyes to find their yurta at the bend of the river, "we live only four miles apart. From a mountain everything appears clearer."

The path grew steeper the nearer they came to Turgen's place, and care had to be taken to avoid loose stones and trees blown down in a storm. But neither Aksa nor Tim lagged behind their host. They were so happy to have all of his attention, so eager for what was coming next, that they could think of a hundred things to say. Aksa especially was very inquisitive.

"Turgen," she asked, "why do you live in the mountains instead of the valley, like us?"

"Why? I don't know myself," Turgen answered. "We Lamuts always prefer to live in the mountains near water. We aren't like the Yakuts who need good grazing grounds for their horses and cows. Look at me. I have nothing except two guns, fishing tackle and my strong legs. I don't even own a dog. Most Lamuts are poor. It seems to be our fate. Besides, there aren't many of us left. Here—I'm the only one. There was another family who lived here several years ago, but they moved."

"Why?" Tim wanted to know.

"I can't say, my boy. Just as a fish seeks deeper water, so a man looks for a place that will be better for him. Only happiness does not lie in changing one place for another, but in belonging to a fine family like yours."

Turgen patted Aksa's head as he spoke.

"Didn't you have a family before?" she questioned.

When Turgen answered her his face was sober. "Yes, but they went away, leaving me alone."

"To what place did they go?" the girl persisted.

But Turgen could not talk about this. "To the place all people must go. It is too soon for you to understand."

Before Aksa could open her mouth for another question, Tim pulled her painfully by her braid, saying, "We are now your family. So Mama said. I will live with you, Turgen, forever."

"And so will I!" Aksa hastened to add.

"Splendid!" Turgen said, the smile coming back to his eyes. "And now that is settled we must get to the end of our journey."

Tim, wanting to distract attention from a subject that was plainly not to Turgen's liking, and also because he was bursting with questions of his own, blurted out: "Is it true what people say, that you are friendly with wild rams?"

When Turgen showed no sign of distaste for this subject, he rushed on: "I can hardly believe that rams will let you come close to them. From what I hear, they run faster than the wind and can jump from one mountain to another. It is difficult even to see them. We have never seen them— not Mama nor Aksa nor I. Are they really so smart that they know of danger before it comes near them? People also say—"

The boy broke off sharply.

"That I am a sorcerer and bewitched. Is that what people say?" Turgen finished for him. But his expression was kind.

Tim nodded. "This we don't believe."

"Good. People will always tak a lot of nonsense when they haven't anything better to do." Turgen shook his head. "More's the pity. But since you are interested I will tell you what I know of the rams. What you hear is part true and part exaggeration. Yes, Lad was my friend. I cannot say as much for the old rams who are still fearful because I am a man. And why should they love us who hunt them down?" Turgen hesitated. "Later I will tell you more. And tomorrow, if you should happen to wake up early, and the day is bright, you will be able to see the rams for yourself on top of that cliff over there." He pointed to the one opposite his yurta.

Aksa and Tim clapped their hands and whirled with joy. "Will you, Turgen? Oh, will you? We will do anything you say, and get up very early."

A sight of the rams was worth any promise.

CHAPTER 24

ANYTHING NEW HAS A SPECIAL WONDER. TIM and Aksa had never been in a yurta like Turgen's before and they had to explore every nook and corner. The mountains hovering over it were giants standing guard. The tiny window which with difficulty let in light might have belonged to a playhouse they built for their own amusement.

Listening to them exclaim and argue and laugh, Turgen prepared dinner. Here and there, in and out, the children ran like busy moles. Secretly they hoped for a glimpse of the mountain rams that same night. Yet they were willing to wait, for Turgen had promised. It would be hard to say whether Turgen or his guests were happier.

Dinner was a feast. There was ukha or fish-soup which they drank out of wooden bowls; there were also fat fish and pheasants roasted on a spit. And to top it all was tea with . . . sugar! Yes, it was a real feast, something to tell their mother about.

Yet the children's real joy that day came not so much from the trip up the mountain and the good food as from the attention Turgen paid them. They were not used to this. Their mother, they knew, loved them, but she was always so busy looking after them that she had little time to play with them. Here was Turgen ready to devote a whole evening and day to them.

And this was not all. They would hear the story of the rams.

Their stomachs so full that it seemed they must burst, Tim and Aksa waited while Turgen cleared away the meal. He then went to the door and stood looking out. They understood that he was hoping for a glimpse of his rams.

"Can't see a thing," he said finally, turning back to the room and closing the door against the cold air. "What do you say to some more logs on the fire?"

The children nodded.

Soon flames were dancing in the komelek; the room was snug and warm. Turgen lit his pipe and smiled at his guests, well pleased with them and the day. He was content now to sit in silence and enjoy the comfort. But not Aksa.

"Turgen, is it true that you are old?" she wanted to

know. Then, seeing him smile, she hastened to add, "Mama says that only your hair is old—that you are strong and walk the earth as lightly as a mountain ram."

Turgen's face showed his pleasure. "A clever girl," he thought, and was not surprised by her next question: "You haven't forgotten your promise to tell us about yourself and the rams?"

He shook his head. "How could I forget? It is all so close to my heart."

With that he began to talk. He started with the time long ago when he had been young and happy; told of his struggles and adventures and marriage. When he came to the death of his wife and son, Aksa and Tim shed tears for him in his loneliness. The next moment they were all smiles again as he described finding the rams who brought new meaning to his life. But most exciting was the account of his remarkable dreams. Here Aksa began to fidget on the bench by the fire and pressed close to Tim, who sat motionless with his mouth open, his unblinking eyes fixed on Turgen.

To them it was not a dream that Turgen had visited the Great Spirit and later entertained him as a mysterious wanderer. They accepted it all as something which had really happened and their admiration for Turgen was unbounded.

"As I see it," Turgen declared in conclusion, "the Great Spirit gave me a love for these rams as a gift for my old age. Then, pleased that I cared for them according to His bidding, He blessed me with a fine family."

The children jumped up, ran to Turgen and embraced him. Their eyes were full of love, their heads full of questions.

"Now, together, we can protect our herd," Turgen said with satisfaction.

"But how?" asked Tim.

"Quite simply," Turgen replied. "We have a custom which says that only one hunter is permitted in a district. As I live and hunt here, and do not molest the rams, they are safe."

"But if you do not come close to them," Tim persisted, "how can you be sure they are the same rams you knew long ago?"

Turgen hesitated. "That I can't know for certain, my boy, but a bird can be followed by its flight, and an animal by its tracks. I saw their tracks more than once. The same family? Maybe. Maybe not. One thing I know well, that rams love to return to their native haunts. Naturally, they avoided me, for how could they know I was their friend? Their life was very difficult."

Aksa's eyes asked a question.

"Why? Food is scarce and the rams have many enemies: people the most dangerous of all. They can fight a wolf, run away from a bear, but a hunter's bullet is faster than their legs. So they hide among the mountain cliffs. And what kind of food is there? In summer, a little grass and a few thin shrubs—in winter, nothing but half-frozen twigs and old dry moss. Not very nourishing. It is no wonder the poor creatures die out."

Tim, who had been listening intently, now blurted out: "I think they must be stupid to live in such places. All they have to do is come to lower ground where there is plenty of food."

"On the contrary," Turgen told him, "they are smart. Where they live there is sand and gravel and loose stones to warn them of the approach of an enemy. Have you ever tried to walk quietly on gravel? . . . Well! The rams had their choice—to live in terror of their lives below where there is food, or to go hungry and free. The dead need nothing. They chose to live and be free. In their independence they remind me of my own people—the Lamuts. We too are dying out, but we are free."

"The poor rams," Aksa commented. "During a snow storm we keep a fire burning day and night, but they have no way to warm themselves."

"Yes," Tim agreed. "And even with fire and food we do not have an easy time of it in winter."

Pleased to have aroused the sympathy of his young guests, Turgen replied, "It is impossible not to pity these fine savages. Fortunately, God has provided them with some things to help them in their struggle. They are strong, have great endurance, and towards winter their wool becomes thick and long. Moreover they are intelligent. You see how I built my yurta between cliffs. In winter everything is so covered with snow that there is not a chink for the wind to enter in. And wind is far more dangerous than frost. The rams know this, so they seek for themselves caves in the mountains where they too will be protected from the wind. Their great misfortune is hunger."

Tim considered a moment. "Is there no way to help them?"

"If we would, yes," Turgen answered. "I have heard that in other countries rare animals are protected by law. It is forbidden to hunt them. But we have no such law, even for animals as rare and harmless as these."

"We could tame them and use them," Tim offered. "One of our neighbors has sheep and I have heard that mountain rams are wild sheep."

Turgen shook his head. "So are dogs related to wolves. But there is a proverb: No matter how much you feed a wolf, he will still long for the woods. I have never seen or heard of a tame wolf. Wild rams are not wolves, but it is impossible to tame them."

"What about Lad? You tamed him," Aksa interrupted.

"That is right. But Lad was very young, and at the time I got him he was helpless. For a time he was satisfied to stay with me, but you should have seen how eagerly he rushed to his father the instant he heard his voice! When I called he turned his head and looked at me. That was all."

"Ah, how ungrateful!" Aksa exclaimed.

"It is not a question of gratitude at all. Imagine that you were lost in the woods and hurt yourself. Someone found you and took care of you. Then suddenly you saw your mother . . . Wouldn't you run to her?"

Aksa's eyes opened wide. "But Mother and I are people," she objected.

"So," Turgen nodded, smiling. "But animals too have a feeling for their own kind."

Tim now came to his sister's defense. "I think Lad should

have stayed with you. Then he would have been warm and well fed."

Turgen answered with a question: "Would you leave your mother who is poor to live in the yurta of a rich neighbor?"

"Oh, no, no!"

"I didn't expect any other answer," Turgen told the boy. "Our own family always comes first. And sooner or later, looking at the mountains, Lad would have been seized with longing to be there with the other mountain rams. Only by force could I have kept him. Then, maybe, by the second or the third generation . . ."

"Why didn't you?" Tim wanted to know.

"Keep him by force? No. Better he should live in freedom." Turgen paused, and added, "Besides, I was afraid."

"Afraid!" Aksa exclaimed in disbelief. "What were you afraid of?"

"The Great Spirit might have been angry," Turgen explained, "had I not given the lamb back to his family. I feared too that the people from below might come and kill him. If they could believe he was a devil in disguise, they could do anything. There in the mountains he is safer. It is where he belongs."

Turgen rose. "Now come. It is time to sleep if you want

to see my rams in the morning. They come to gather on that near cliff at sunrise."

After a day of such excitements, with the hope of more to come, the children had hardly time to cover themselves with blankets and quickly say a prayer than they were asleep. Turgen did not follow them immediately but sat smoking by the fire. His face reflected joy in his new fortune. In his heart too was a prayer.

"I thank Thee for the gift of this fine family, and for your goodness to my rams who are also dear to me. Teach people to let them live in peace. For nothing is impossible to Thee."

CHAPTER 25

TURGEN WAS WAKENED NEXT MORNING BY the cold rushing in through the chimney of the now dead komelek. He jumped out of bed, revived the fire, put water to boil for tea and then stepped out of the yurta.

Before him were the mountains enveloped in a thick white-gray fog. He peered in the direction of the cliff where he expected the rams, but could see nothing. Anxiously he waited. They must come! The fog must lift! He had promised the children.

When the rising sun sent its first golden threadlike rays into the sky, slowly, slowly the fog moved up the mountains. Fearing to miss a moment Turgen shouted from the door of the yurta: "Tim! Aksa! Get up! It is time!"

The children scrambled from their beds and still in their bare feet rushed to join Turgen. With eyes opened wide to miss nothing of the spectacle, they saw for the first time day break over the mountains. It was a dazzling sight. And as the mist gave way before the power of the sun, there were the rams—shadowy silhouettes, then the whole herd seen sharp and clear.

The leader was standing in front by himself, with the others ranged around him. They were posed as for a show.

"Look," Turgen was saying. "There beside the old fellow is my Lad. See, he is looking straight at us. I am certain he has told them about us."

"Oh, they are beautiful!" Aksa exclaimed.

To her, their beauty was enough. But Tim's thoughts went farther. "I hope they will always come to this mountain," he said.

"They will if we care for them and love them," Turgen assured him.

The three stood without moving, watching as the leader ram signalled to the herd and led them down the mountain out of sight. Even then they were reluctant to let the moment go. The rams and the mountain against the red-gold sky was something to keep forever.

Tim broke the silence, and his voice was a little sad: "Eh, Turgen, I do want them to live in health so that we can enjoy them if only from a distance. God save them from hunger and cold and wild beasts and hunters."

"So long as I live," Turgen answered, "they will eat well and be safe from hunters. But what will become of them after I die? This is my worry."

Impulsively Tim caught Turgen by the arm. "Then I will feed and protect them. I promise you."

"And I, and I, too!" Aksa exclaimed.

Turgen put his arm around the children. "Wonderful!" he said. "You make me very happy. Feed the rams, love and protect them. The Good Spirit will reward you for it, as He has rewarded me."

Indeed, at that moment Turgen felt himself to be the happiest of men.

CHAPTER 26

WINGS OF HAPPINESS LIFTED TURGEN'S spirit in the days immediately following his understanding with Marfa, until it seemed that the world was a new and more beautiful place. He looked at the sky, the mountains and the forest around him with eyes that appeared to see them for the first time. Even his yurta, so dark and cramped, was larger and brighter, though its solitary window was still covered with snow. In the silence surrounding him he caught sounds of life filled with excitement and promise.

"Is not all this a dream?" he asked himself. Then his common sense answered: "No, it is not a dream, or there would be fear in my heart that it would vanish. And my heart does not fear."

He was very gay as he climbed the mountain to the clearing with food for his rams. The herd kept out of sight, but he felt their presence close by in the shelter of the cliffs.

"Hey there, my friends," he shouted, "don't hide yourselves!" And then, because he had to confide his news to someone: "Life has now turned her face to us and everything is going to be well. We are no longer orphans. I will have a family, and it will be your family, too. Already Tim and Aksa love you. And they have made me a promise. As for their mother! Oh, that is a woman with a heart. The Great Spirit has blessed us indeed."

Turgen delivered his message with full confidence that the rams heard and understood all that he said, and rejoiced in his good fortune. He knew the proverb, "Every man forges his own happiness," but his case seemed to be an exception. For what had he done, he asked himself, that he should be so blessed? Was it all, perhaps, a sign from the stranger who came to him in his dream?

For three days his thoughts were rose-colored. But no mood will last forever. Gradually doubts crept back into his mind and by feeding on solitude grew into monsters.

"What kind of an old fool am I to be thinking of marriage at my age?" they went. "How do I dare take on the responsibility of a family? Not that I am unable to provide for them. But why should innocent people have to share with me the ill-will of the Yakuts in the valley?"

Marfa was a fine brave woman. She and the children scoffed at the idea that he was a sorcerer. But they didn't know what it meant to have their neighbors against them.

What was he to do? How could he explain all this to Marfa and make her understand that his fears were for her and not himself?

That was the whole problem—to convince Marfa. It would require wisdom. And where was he to find wisdom of the kind needed? Oh, what a muddle it was, and all because of his pity for the mountain rams. How was it possible that so much evil could come from good?

While his mind worried itself in this fashion Turgen went about his daily chores hoping that the Great Spirit would grant him still another sign, and save him before the final moment of decision. There was much work to be done. There were the fishing nets in the lake to watch. There was game to be hunted, and snares to be examined from time to time. Also he had promised to sew new moccasin boots for Tim and Aksa. Then on the following Sunday he would return to Marfa's, when she expected to decide upon the day for the wedding.

What this wedding would be like Turgen did not know.

He remembered very well his first marriage, which had taken place early in the autumn. Several couples gathered outside the chapel and were united by one ceremony. There was a small table holding a cross and a bowl of water. A person called a monk read a prayer, sprinkled holy water over them, and invited them to kiss the cross. Then a man wearing glasses wrote down their names— and that was all. This had been long ago—so long ago. How would it be now if Marfa was not persuaded by his reasoning?

It was good to be busy, for then he could not think too much.

CHAPTER 27

EARLY SATURDAY MORNING KAMOV WAS DUE TO call with provisions. Turgen knew that he had a credit with the merchant amounting to more than three hundred roubles. Add to this the value of the pelts he had on hand, and the sum would be about five hundred roubles. A lot of money. It would buy not only necessary supplies but dress goods for Marfa and the children.

"It might be well also," he thought, "to get another cow and a good horse." For though he reasoned with himself against the marriage, he could not give up hope. The merchant was a man to be trusted. He would ask his advice.

That night Turgen tossed in his sleep and his dreams were troubled. He dozed, wakened, dozed again and heard himself mutter: "But I cannot let the poor creatures starve in order to convince stupid people that I am not a friend of the devil. What kind of happiness would I have? No and no!"

And then to his surprise he saw Lad at the door of the yurta, looking at him with affection and saying in a human voice: "Why don't you sleep, Turgen? You know that I and my parents, and indeed the entire herd, are praying for you. Sleep. All will be well."

Turgen sprang from his bed, rubbed his eyes and looked around the yurta. No one was there. Logs crackled in the komelek, the room was warm and snug. Stepping outside the door he looked at the moon and stars, worlds away, making bright patterns in the night-black sky. A wonder, but distant from his thoughts just now. "Merciful God," he whispered as he turned back, "what is wrong with me? Am I ill that such strange things haunt me?"

Suddenly something came over him, a feeling of peace and well-being which seemed to promise that though he could not know the answers to all his questioning, they would be revealed in good time. The Great Spirit was on guard and would see to it. So, reassured, he fell asleep.

When Kamov arrived in the morning, Turgen greeted him cordially and set about preparing refreshments. Outwardly he was calm but he had difficulty keeping mind on what the merchant was saying. Once he caught himself hanging an empty kettle over the fire, and nothing he wanted was in its usual place.

Kamov could not help noticing Turgen's distraction. Perhaps the man was ill—worried. To live too much alone was bad. The merchant respected the Lamut and liked him. He remembered with gratitude how once Turgen had cured him of acute stomach pains, and he would return the favor if he could. But it is not the habit of northern people to pry. There is a right and a wrong time to ask questions.

So the two men ate while they exchanged news of no importance. Afterwards they settled back to enjoy their pipes. From behind a cloud of smoke Kamov spoke.

"You know, Turgen, you have a considerable sum of money with me. Hundreds of roubles. Why don't you spend some of it?"

"Yes . . . Well . . . I have everything I need. . . ." Turgen stopped, not knowing how to tell the merchant what was in his mind. "However, I have been thinking of making quite a large purchase."

Kamov saw that the conversation was taking an important turn. Cautiously feeling his way, he said:

"I mention this because we are living at God's mercy. If I should die, no one would know how much I owe you.

For I carry everything in my head. You know yourself that most of the hunters are in my debt. And your case is special. I should not like to go before God owing you so much. It happens that I have brought with me a great deal of merchandise. Friend, take as much as you like."

"Why talk of death?" Turgen answered. "May God grant you many summers and winters of life in good health. It is already more than thirty winters that I have been dealing with you and I am not complaining. Besides, who of us knows whose turn will come first?"

Kamov sighed, "Nor am I complaining. My health and business are very good. I won't hide it from you. I make a fair profit, and without cheating. Maybe that is why God has blessed me with a comfortable living and a fine family. I am surprised that you go on living alone. It must be hard—ay?"

It was this question that Turgen needed to unlock his thoughts. He took a long pull at his pipe before he replied: "It is difficult, very difficult. But a change is about to take place in my life . . ."

Carefully he told the merchant all about Marfa and the children, and how happy he would be to have a family except that he feared the ill-will of the Yakuts in the valley would spoil everything.

"You know yourself," he concluded, "that I am not a sorcerer. I believe in God. I had thought to purchase quite a lot of your wares, also to ask where I could get a good horse and cow. Then my household would be complete. But what about this feeling about me? What was bad before will be doubly bad if I have a family. I want to explain all this to Marfa, but I don't know how. God forbid, she might think me a coward and afraid of responsibility. You are a wise man . . . what do you advise?"

Kamov leisurely emptied the ashes from his pipe, was silent a moment and then said:

"You ask for advice? I'll give it gladly. But this matter isn't as simple as it seems. It needs explaining. Yes, I've heard the gossip about you—such lies I wonder anyone can believe them. You should have spoken to me before. Why didn't you?"

"I don't know," Turgen admitted. "But a man is ashamed to be thought a partner of the devil."

Kamov scratched the back of his head as he considered this.

"It is and it isn't a matter for laughing. When I was young and a hunter, a bear once rumpled me badly. But the wounds healed long ago and now I feel no pain at all.

Yet human tongues speaking evil can inflict wounds no medicines will heal . . ."

He paused, filled his pipe and lit it. Suddenly a smile broke over his face. "My friend, I have found a way out for you! Why didn't I think of it before? It is so very simple."

Excited, Turgen jumped to his feet. "Then tell me. Help me."

"Of course . . . of course," Kamov said reassuringly.

He rose, paced back and forth for a minute, and stroked his forehead as if gathering his thoughts together.

"Turgen, you know that the Yakuts are like children. It is easy to lead them astray with lying words. But no one can doubt that they believe in God and fear the devil. No one. They are all Christians even though many of them still run to the shamanists. It was the shamanist who did you the greatest harm—because he was jealous of you. The people came to you for advice and to be cured and you helped them without charge. This took business away from him."

"Maybe," Turgen admitted.

"Believe me, it was so," Kamov said positively. "And for that reason the shamanist spread foolish tales about you— how with the devil's help you were able to make friends with the mountain rams. The simple people could believe such nonsense because rams are known to hate the scent of human beings—so why would they eat the food you brought? . . . No, the Yakuts are stupid no doubt, but not evil. They just believed the first thing they heard. Now—"

Kamov paused dramatically.

"My idea is this. The Yakuts are Christians. They believe in God. You and Marfa are Christians. That being so, you must be married in the Christian manner. You see how simple it is. Once you are joined in God's temple by a priest, who will sprinkle you with holy water and give you the Gospel and the Cross to touch, not a soul will dare to say that you are a friend of the devil. Believe me, faith and prayer—they are the best answer to slander. Do you understand?"

Turgen nodded. "I feel that you speak the truth, Kamov. Tell me, what must I do? Go to a priest? That will be about sixty miles, but I can do it easily on my skis. What shall I say to him? I have never in my life had anything to do with a priest. And this is a delicate subject . . . Teach me, my friend!"

Kamov patted Turgen on the shoulder, pleased to have his advice so well received. "Don't excite yourself. You need do nothing. I will see to everything myself. The priest is a friend of mine. You will make a donation to the church and pay the trifling expenses—that is all. Thank God you are not a poor man . . . And now we must set a day for the wedding. What would you say to Sunday, two weeks from now? Time is needed for preparations, and I want to spread news of the wedding among the valley people. Father Peter, as you know, is greatly respected. I shall tell the Yakuts, too," Kamov added with a sly wink, "that I will be your best man. Popov can give the bride away. Everyone looks up to him, and besides he lives close to the chapel. Do you agree?"

"I agree to everything. Thank you. Thank you," said Turgen gratefully.

"Well, then, all is settled. Just don't say anything to Marfa. I will see Popov at once, and arrange for a party at his house after the wedding. He's a good man and I do a lot of business with him. He won't refuse. About the cow— we will buy that from Popov. One hand washes the other, you know." Here Kamov winked at Turgen again. "As for the horse, that will be my present, as best man, to you. But there is one thing I ask of you."

"Yes, yes," Turgen interrupted. "Anything."

"I know that you are not a drinking man, Turgen. Perhaps you do not approve of others drinking. But the Yakuts will not think it possible to celebrate an occasion as important as a wedding without both prayer and vodka. Nothing too gay because you aren't young any more. Just enough to wet their throats and lighten their hearts."

Turgen smiled. "Why not? I have no objection. I do not drink because many years ago I took a little too much of the poison, and when returning home I lost my way, fell into a hole and almost froze to death. That experience taught me a lesson, and I promised my wife that never again would I touch a drop of the stuff. However, it is not for me to sit in judgment upon others. Our guests must be free to do as they please."

"Good!" Kamov exclaimed. "That's a sensible and just way to look at it."

Kamov remembered at this point that his horses had not been fed or watered.

"It's a pull up the mountain, too," he explained, "though fortunately the snow is not deep. Come help me bring the merchandise indoors where you can examine it. If I don't have everything you want with me, I'll get it from my store and send it direct to Marfa."

As Turgen selected from Kamov's stores all the things he wanted for Marfa and the children and the new home they would have together there was joy in his heart. Thinking of the pleasure his purchases would bring, he considered that he was performing one of the most important acts of his lifetime. And this feeling of exaltation stayed with him long after Kamov had left.

"No, the world is not lacking in kind people," he reflected. "How good it is to open one's heart to a friend." Truly it was a miracle that the Great Spirit had sent Lad in the night with the promise that all would be well. And how comforting to know that he, Turgen, did not bear his responsibility alone, but that Someone greater and wiser than he commanded his life.

He did his chores that evening as if wings lent lightness to his feet. After emptying the nets and snares of game, he rushed to feed his rams. "Eh, my darlings, if you could only know how happy I am!" he called. But the herd did not show itself.

Then before re-entering his yurta, he stopped by the grave of his wife and son. "Long ago you went away from me, but still you are close," he addressed them, and his words were a prayer. "This is the place above all places where I find peace. I have come to you often with my grief, so now let me come to you with my joy. Give me your blessing, that I am to be alone no longer. What have I done to deserve this I do not know, but who does know the Great Spirit or the extent of His generosity? May His grace be with us all, forever."

Such a day must be concluded in a fitting manner, so Turgen got out his reed and played and played until it seemed the walls of the yurta could not contain so much melody. He sang of hope and joy and beauty and peace of soul. And finally he slept dreamlessly, hearing still the music of his own creation.

CHAPTER 28

THE NEXT TWO WEEKS SPED BY. THERE WERE visits to Marfa and the children, plans to be made and discussed. And several times Kamov called to report cheerfully that everything he had undertaken to do was progressing splendidly.

According to him, the people of the valley were at first completely overwhelmed by his news. "Have you heard? Turgen is going to marry the poor widow Marfa." The word spread like fire. What seemed to occasion surprise was not that Marfa was marrying a Lamut, but that Turgen was taking upon himself the burden of providing for her and the children.

Once that fact was accepted, everyone—men and women—had something to say about the wedding. A real wedding, in their own small chapel, with a service performed by Father Peter himself. And after the ceremony— greatest marvel of all—there was to be a feast in the yurta of the Bailiff Popov, with the doors open to rich and poor, young and old. The people of the valley boiled with excitement and amazement. "Just think of it, Father Peter himself will marry them! What a blessing! The Father will travel sixty miles just for that! Such an event does not occur every day."

Gradually, in the eyes of the people, Turgen was becoming a highly respected man, and Marfa, a fortunate woman to get him for her husband. She was younger than he, but that was considered no obstacle so long as a man was strong and not bad looking. Moreover, Turgen was well-to-do. The woman who got him, said the wives sagely, would not have to work hard.

Public opinion was so strongly in Turgen's favor that when someone mentioned carelessly his friendship with the devil, the gossiper was hissed into silence. "Keep your mouth shut," bystanders ordered him. "Would the priest have consented to give his blessing if what you say were true? No. How is it possible that a sorcerer could cross the threshold of a chapel? No and No. People were just talking nonsense."

Only the shamanist failed to express an opinion. Those who tried to seek him out and question him were put off by the woman Stepa who announced with authority, "The great shamanist is ill and unable to talk." But she gave it as a fact that he had nothing against the marriage.

This was enough to convince the shamanist's ardent supporters that they were free to approve Turgen's action and attend the wedding. Their approval was strengthened daily by rumors of important Yakuts who would be among the guests. And outweighing all else was the fact that Kamov would be best man. The merchant was held in such excellent regard that any project he supported must surely be above suspicion.

"As long as Kamov is his friend, who dares to be Turgen's enemy?" the Yakuts asked of one another. And so the word was passed along and the day of the wedding arrived.

CHAPTER 29

FROM EARLY MORNING A LARGE CROWD OF men, women, and children gathered near the chapel. At the hour set for the ceremony a sigh of approval went up as ten sleighs appeared drawn by white horses whose tails and manes were braided with multicolored ribbons. Around the animals' necks tinkling bells were hung, and their harnesses were dazzling.

"Not a bishop or a governor would be ashamed of such horses," said one watcher to another.

In the first sleigh, driven by the eminent Popov, rode the priest with his psalmist, at sight of whom the men uncovered their heads and the women bowed low. Behind the priest rode Turgen with Kamov. Then came Marfa with the children and the wife of Popov. And behind them notables of the district with their wives.

It was a real procession, grand enough to satisfy the

most critical. Even nature rejoiced. The sun was out and the snow sparkled under its rays.

The priest descending blessed the people, the chapel's single bell boomed out, and the guests crossed themselves as they knelt.

With difficulty everyone crowded into the small chapel, for no one wanted to miss this most unusual event. There was a feeling of expectation and awe.

Blessing the people again, the priest began to pray:

"Brothers, sisters, let us pray to the Lord God for all our people and for the prosperity of our great land."

It was a brief prayer, and after that the wedding service started.

Turgen felt himself to be in a trance. Never before in his life had he been the center of so much attention. The burning candles and the singing moved him to wonder: "Is it possible that all this is for me, a poor Lamut? What have I done to deserve such grace from God?"

He was in fear of making an awkward movement that would mar the service. But the priest lent him support with his kind, understanding eyes, and from time to time when the questions were incomprehensible, Kamov came to his assistance. Marfa beside him was solemn and composed as she whispered what seemed to be a prayer, but when their glances met her face lighted with a smile of quiet happiness.

To the children it was all part of an enchanting fairy tale. This was what their mother meant when she said that Turgen would become their father! It was no more than fitting, of course, that he should be paid such honor. For was not Turgen the greatest of storytellers and the kindest of men? So thinking, they crossed themselves fervently.

Still in a daze, unable either to think or to pray in such magnificent surroundings, Turgen got through the ceremony, made a sign opposite his name in a big book, and was taken to the home of the Popovs, where the tables groaned under mountains of food. There was frozen and smoked fish, steaming hot soup, slabs of venison and other meats, and finally delicious cloud-berry with frozen cream.

After a few tumblers of vodka, the place was filled with friends who slapped him on the back and showered him with good wishes. Fortunately, Kamov noted his embarrassment and saved him from the noisiest guests, while at the same time he saw to it that the supply of vodka was limited. There was enough for gayety—and no more. The presence of the priest also was a sobering influence.

It was much later and time for the party to end when Kamov rose and called for silence.

"Friends," he said, "let us wish Turgen, Marfa and the children a long and happy life. There is a custom among us to give gifts to the newlyweds, and for my part I am giving them a fine horse, with harness and sleigh. I hope they will do me the honor to travel to their home in it this night."

He was about to say something more, hesitated and then exclaimed: "Hail to the new family!"

The company broke into enthusiastic applause. "Fine, fine! Okse! Okse!" It was an excellent speech, everyone agreed. No one could have done better.

Not to be outdone by the merchant, Popov now got to his feet: "And I am making the new family a present of one of my best milk cows."

Others, stirred to generosity by the prevailing good will, shouted above the hubbub declaring their gifts. Afterwards all trooped out to the yard to see Turgen off, on the invitation of Kamov who longed to hear the horse and sleigh admired.

After seeing that Marfa and the children were made comfortable for the ride, Turgen took his seat and to the accompaniment of gay, friendly voices urged the horse into motion. Soon the voices were left behind. The forest closed in on either side and there was nothing to be heard but the pounding hoofs, the creak of runners, and the cheerful tinkle of a bell around the horse's neck.

Marfa touched Turgen's arm. "It is like a dream," she said. "Such kind people."

There were many things Turgen might have said in answer. But why remember evil? So he only looked at his wife and smiled.

Aksa, who had been unusually silent, now spoke up: "Turgen—Tim and I have decided to call you Father. May we?"

"Indeed you may," Turgen responded heartily. "And just when did you decide this?"

"Oh, as soon as we left the church."

Turgen nodded. "I see. So that is settled and I suppose," he added slyly, "you have no other problems."

"Yes, I have," she retorted. "I want to know what we are going to call this horse."

Turgen deliberated.

"Would Friend be a good name?"

"Yes, very good!" the girl exclaimed.

Tim, impatient with his bold, talkative sister, could hold in no longer. "It seems to me we have a great many animals. But to whom will the mountain rams belong?"

Turgen felt a surge of love for the boy. Half-jokingly and

half-seriously he answered: "Yes, we have the beginning of a fine household. But the rams belong to God, and they will always be His. You and I can only guard and care for them. You remember you promised."

Then, his heart so full of happiness that he did not trust his voice to express it, he grasped the reins and shouted to the horse: "Come Friend. Hurry! We are going home."

The horse quickened its pace, the children shrieked in pleasure, Marfa and Turgen looked at each other and smiled. Not one of them doubted that they were rushing full speed toward a new and a good life.

CHAPTER 30

SINCE THAT DAY MANY YEARS HAVE PASSED. TURgen and Marfa saw the children grow up, and as the children grew their own well-being increased. Wealth was never theirs, but they had enough for their wants, and any visitor was assured of a welcome place by their fire.

The Yakuts, conscious of their guilt before Turgen, did their best to make up for their past behavior and show their respect. Even the shamanist, now very old, came one day to beg forgiveness. When Turgen said to him, "We'll forget the past. Come and be my guest," the shamanist was so touched that he told everyone "Turgen is one of the kindest of men. There is more wisdom in his little finger than in my old head."

So the old injustice was buried.

Gradually others came to settle near Marfa's yurta, until

a large settlement sprang up around the lake. As they planned, Turgen and his family lived in the valley during the winter and in the mountains during the summer. Though a great change had come into his life, he did not forget his rams but cared for them as before. When age made him feebler, he had a fine assistant in Tim who was young and strong.

Turgen lived to see his Lad the leader of a herd of his own. Then one day, not long after Tim was married, he departed quietly for the other world where Marfa had already gone.

"Do not forget my poor rams and God will be merciful to you," were the last words he spoke.

Tim and Aksa were faithful to their promise. In time there were four herds in the mountains instead of one. And the rams no longer fled pell-mell at the sight of human beings. Perhaps, as Turgen believed, this was because of Lad and the things he had learned during the period of his accident. Whatever the explanation, the rams of this region lived in peace and flourished, while the people too knew comfort and abundance. Surely the Great Spirit, who saw all, had given His blessing.

* * *

So it was that I, a visitor by accident to Turgen's mountain country, found proof that my teacher spoke truly when he said: "Everywhere there is life and everywhere there are warm human hearts."